The Secret Letters of Mama Cat

also by Jody Sorenson

To Take Your Heart Away
Waiting
Playing Games
Settling the Score

The Secret Letters of Mama Cat

Jody Sorenson

Walker and Company
New York

First published in the United States of America in 1988 by the Walker Publishing
Company, Inc.

Published simultaneously in Canada by Thomas Allen & Son
Canada, Limited, Markham, Ontario.

Library of Congress Cataloging-in-Publication Data

Sorenson, Jody.
    The secret letters of mama cat.

    Summary: During her first year in junior high, Meredith deals with several crises, in-
cluding moving to Texas, the departure of her sister to a boarding school for the deaf, and
the death of her grandmother.
    [1. Grandmothers—Fiction. 2. Death—Fiction. 3. Moving, Household—Fiction.
4. Deaf—Fiction] I. Title.
PZ7.S72145Se 1988   [Fic]   87-25333
ISBN 0-8027-6779-6
ISBN 0-8027-6791-5 (reinf.)

Printed in the United States of America

10 9 8 7 6 5 4 3 2 1

Book design by Laurie McBarnette

In thanksgiving for my grandmother
Ada Sorenson

Chapter ● 1 ●

I set my arms Indian fashion across my chest. "Dr. Goldstein has the plaster cast of my mouth and I won't move to Texas. Not now. We've waited this long. Can't we wait for a better time, like till my braces come off?" With the tip of my tongue I checked the hole my bottom braces had made on the inside of my lip. I was always having to check it for food that would get trapped there. I could pull out my lower lip, and if I got the angle just right the food would pop out. I liked to look in the bathroom mirror when I did that, though. Besides, it bothered my parents.

"We'll have him send the cast to an orthodontist in San Antonio." My father stopped eating his lunch and sat forward. He's a lawyer, a very logical lawyer, and sometimes he makes me feel like I'm one of his cases. My mom's a lawyer too, but different. She's different from all of us because her last name is Malone. The rest of us are McGees. I tell everyone my parents never married. That kind of news makes life more exciting.

"It's not fair," I protested. "School starts in less than three weeks. I don't want to go to school someplace else."

"A promotion's been a possibility for nearly a year," my father

1

said, "and we all knew that it would mean a move. We've talked about it. And now they won't wait any longer to have me take over the legal affairs department down there. They're desperate."

"But please not now. Not so soon before school's supposed to start. I've got my clothes and my classes all set up with Jeannie. Everything's planned for here." My throat tightened. Getting ready to go to junior high was hard enough without moving too. "You didn't give me a good enough warning." I felt hurt somehow. Maybe it was about not being better warned. Maybe it was because my father never seemed to understand how important some things were to me, like clothes and friends.

"It's good timing if you ask me," Mom began.

"But nobody asked *me,*" I said. I knew I was getting way out of line arguing as I was, but I didn't stop. "You just waited till Grandma died, that's all. When it comes to me you don't think. Just because Tina doesn't hear and Adam doesn't care doesn't mean I'm not here. I count." I was glad that Tina, who's three years older than I, wasn't home yet. She was at a creative-arts camp for the deaf on Lake Michigan. I went to day camp and it finished yesterday. I didn't end up with a boyfriend like I hoped. Adam's only three and he doesn't care much about anything except maybe getting everyone's attention and making a mess.

"Of course you count." Mom leaned forward further than Dad, and I sat as far back in my chair as I could. "The move will be a good change for all of us. Mac has been hoping for this for a long time, and then when Grandma died it did become easier to make the move."

"I count too," Adam exclaimed. "One, two, three . . ."

I stopped listening, going as deaf as Tina. I could tell we were going to move, and suddenly I didn't feel like making my point anymore. My father says I'll make a good lawyer someday, the way I argue my side. I don't know. Whenever my heart's bothered, like it still was about Grandma, I can't continue doing anything, especially talking hard and fast.

"It's okay," I said. I took a bite of tuna sandwich, which I couldn't swallow. My throat began to close. I hated to get that way in front of people. "Can I be excused?"

"Sure," Mom answered.

I could feel my father nod. I didn't want to look at him. I walked to the kitchen, put down my plate and ran to my bedroom.

Several minutes later there was a knock at the door. "Meredith?" It was my mom.

"Yeah?"

"Can I come in?"

"Sure."

"Are you okay?"

"Sure." That wasn't exactly true. I felt very out of sorts lately, and it had nothing to do with the news we would soon be moving.

"We're going to pick up Tina. Do you want to come along?"

"No. I have some things to do. I have to call Jeannie and tell her the bad news."

Mom came and sat on my bed. She didn't say anything. She patted my head for a few minutes, until Dad hollered from the front door. As she rose to join him she said, "Maybe you can take horseback-riding lessons in Texas."

This wasn't a promise that seemed to make any difference to me as I lay on my bed while they were gone. I was thinking about Grandma, and how moving to Texas would take me just that much further from her.

When everyone was home again Adam opened my door. "Come play."

"When are you going to learn to knock?"

"Cowboys don't knock."

"You a cowboy?"

"Yeah. 'Cause of Texas. But I'd rather play 'Mama Cat, Baby Cat.' Come play. Please." In this new game I played the mama cat who looked for the lost baby cat.

"Okay." Playing with Adam almost always made me feel good.

My folks and Tina were in the living room. We all know sign language except Adam, who can barely communicate in one language yet, and I stood for a moment in the doorway watching how excited she looked as she signed, her long fingers flashing. Her hands were beautiful and lively. Grandma had called them hands that could heal, their expression was so graceful. I wondered why she was so excited, but I didn't stay to find out. Adam was far ahead of me and I raced to follow him out the kitchen door and down the back stairway to the playground our building has for the kids who live there. Instead of searching for my lost baby cat— Adam—I dashed for a swing.

"I'm so angry." I knew I had no power to change my parents' plans, but I couldn't stop feeling angry. I hit my feet into dry dirt beneath the swing and dust swirled into the air, making me feel somehow better. What the world needed was a good destruction. I breathed out one of my fireballs. "Aaah . . ."

"Don't do that!" Adam yelled at me. I don't think Adam knows much about life at all. But when he was born I caught this gleam in his eyes that made me feel he knew everything and was just taking his time. I wondered, too, if maybe in some ways I knew more when I was a baby than I do now. That wondering is too weird to explain to anyone, so I keep that thought to myself as much as possible. Sometimes when the thought creeps in I act like it isn't there, like I'm too weird even for myself.

"Why not?" I yelled back. "You'd be angry too if you were

having to give up friends." I breathed out another fireball, one to blow up the whole garage. I had imagined people could have fireballs one day while watching Tina explain how a teacher had insulted her. She was angry. All her feelings leap right out from her hands and face, but anger does that even more. It's part of how she communicates. To me she looked as if she were tossing fireballs and staring fireballs and making them explode all around her.

"Don't do that!" Adam's curly blond head bobbed closer to me and then he stopped.

"It's okay," I said to reassure him. I could tell I was scaring him, and that made me feel even more selfish about being so disagreeable about moving. "They're not real anyway. They're like the fire-breathing dragon stories Grandma used to tell. Remember? They were just pretend."

"They're real. And scary."

"No. It's all pretend. I bet I can make pretty ones too." In my mind I created a fireball that was lovely, peachy, and baby blue. It looked like a colored fountain, and that startled me because once in a while my grandmother would talk about people as fountains: dry or flowing, bitter or sweet. "But I won't even do that." I went back to swinging, in a quiet sort of way, while Baby Cat Adam got himself lost. Eventually I'd rush to his rescue. But for the moment I was starting to think again about Grandma and the nice birthday letter she'd written me.

My grandmother died in June, two weeks before my twelfth birthday. But she still had a card and a letter and some money ready for me. Mom said that's how special I was to her, so special she didn't want to miss celebrating my birthday, no matter what. While Tina has always seemed to have Mom's attention, and Adam, because he's a boy, my father's special interest, I in the middle always had Grandma on my side.

I wanted to say thanks for the card and money in person, but

I couldn't anymore. So, weird though it sounds, even weirder than weird, I wrote her a thank-you note.

I wanted to ask her about fountains and how she got her ideas about them. In my birthday card she wished my fountain many blessings. It's a wish the wise make in the Bible, in the book of Proverbs, which talks a lot about water and fountains. But even the Bible didn't help me understand any better where my fountain is or why it should be blessed. Grandma read from Proverbs and Psalms every day, and something from the New Testament too, and I was sorry she wasn't here to help me understand. There were lots of other things I wanted to say, because she was very special to me. Anyway, it always felt good to talk to her and writing the note felt good, too.

So after dinner I went to the drugstore and bought a spiral notebook with a big butterfly on front. And I wrote another letter to Grandma that night. I needed the good feelings that being with my grandmother always gave me.

August 23

Dear Grandma,

Can you believe it? We're moving to San Antonio, Texas. The news still has me upset. I don't think it's the greatest timing. Besides, I've never lived any place except in our co-op in Chicago.

Please come along, Grandma. There will be lots of new things to share. And no one's as fun as you.

I miss you a lot. I hope I don't miss you more because of the move. Are you homesick for me, too?

Love,
Meredith

P.S. When I'm an adult I'm not going to be like my parents.
I won't let things be changed all around just because they
aren't in the picture anymore.

In the morning I wrote another letter. It felt great to write to
her like that and I decided to write more.

But the letters would have to be my secret. Who in the world,
except my grandma of course, would understand?

Chapter • 2 •

Nothing too exciting happened during the drive to Texas, though Dad did get a ticket during a rainstorm in Dallas when we slid into a car at a stoplight. I wasn't sure I'd ever seen him make a mistake out in public and I watched him like a hawk. I thought he handled himself pretty well. He didn't yell at me or anyone else. Mom said the police officer was as charming and handsome as Rhett Butler. I really didn't pay any attention to the police officer. Dad was not particularly charming with the rain coming in the window, but I've always thought he was handsome.

Sometimes, during the trip, I imagined Grandma sitting quiet in the corner of the back seat. I wanted to write her another letter saying thanks for coming, but I couldn't risk it. As usual, I was right in the middle of the back seat, between Tina and Adam, and they're both snoopy. With them I don't get any privacy.

I liked the motel Mom and Dad picked out for us to stay in while they looked for a house to rent in San Antonio. Out front, by the highway, there was a fake lighthouse with a pulsing beacon, and we had our own kitchen.

Everywhere there were palm trees and I liked them too. They seemed special. Most were tall but there were some short, squat

9

ones at the motel, and I found out that the palm fronds were a lot like porcupine quills. I wanted to cut one down and then I'd have it to shake at whoever bothered me.

At the motel I still didn't have much privacy. I tried to use my suitcase as a desk in the bathroom, locked of course, to tell Grandma how happy I felt sensing her squeezed into our car on the way to Texas.

"Let me in," Adam cried, for probably the tenth time. I think he has a way of knowing the instant when he's not wanted someplace.

"All right, all right." We were never supposed to lock bathroom doors. I did it once when I was four and then couldn't figure out how to unlock it. My father says he spent hours solving that problem, so he made the rule. I slipped my notebook back into my suitcase, unlocked the door, and walked past Adam with my head held high, imitating a palm tree and wishing I did have one under my arm to shake at him.

"We found a house." Dad signed with his hands and spoke at the same time. We were all seated around the dinette for dinner that night. We sign and speak everything. That's called total communication. It's so automatic that lots of times we sign when Tina's not even around. That night we were eating some pretty tasty Southern fried chicken from a take-out next door to the motel.

"So soon?" For the sake of my privacy I wanted a house, but I had hoped for several more days at the motel pool.

"We've only got a few days till school starts," Mom explained.

My stomach flip-flopped and food no longer had the same appeal.

As soon as Tina and Mom began to clear away the dishes I went and sat by the swimming pool. I had sat by the pool the night before and a warm and very gentle breeze had come up as the setting sun turned the sky orange and hot pink. It was a soft breeze, yet exciting. The breeze was company and I wanted to see if it visited every night.

That night, though, I had other company. "Hi," said a girl in the water who was wearing goggles. She reminded me of a frog the way her elbows and knees poked out everywhere. She pulled off her goggles and smiled. Her teeth, perfect and shiny white, made her freckled face seem not so pale. She was a redhead and I figured she probably never dared to get a tan.

"Hi," I answered back.

"Are you coming in?"

"Do I look like I'm coming in?"

"Betcha can't swim."

"Can too."

"Can't." Goggles and snorkle disappeared and I was sprayed by a flipper slapped against the water. Froglike legs bounced spasmodically against the glassy surface. I moved my chair further away from the pool. "So?" she asked. When I didn't respond, she awkwardly lifted herself from the water. She was about my size, a little shorter. She was absolutely flat-chested and she pulled her bikini top up as soon as she landed. She reached for her glasses. After that, she didn't squint at me quite so much when she asked me questions. Questions seemed to be her way of making conversation. She was bold for such a thin, pale person.

"So what?" I asked back.

"So are you going to put on your suit?"

"No." I lay back on the chaise lounge and tried to act like I was from Chicago and very sophisticated.

"Nice sandals."

"Thanks. They're from Marshall Field's."

"Where?"

"Chicago." I liked them too—gold lamé flats with few straps. I didn't tell her my mom had gotten them before we left to help me think positively about moving—I could wear sandals for a lot longer time in Texas. She didn't need to know I was the kind of kid who needed bribing to cooperate. "What's your name?" I asked.

"Charlotte Ann."

"Are you on vacation?"

"No," she answered.

"Do you sneak in at night?"

"No. I live here."

"No kidding." My ears were being charmed and hypnotized by her Texas accent. Words seemed to be shaped at the back of her mouth and deep in her throat, then rounded out in a lovely way. When she said "r" it sounded like "ah."

"We live in back."

"Like a regular family?"

"I guess. My parents are divorced."

"Do you have sisters and brothers?"

"Sort of."

I thought that was a strange answer. "How can you sort of have sisters and brothers?"

"It feels that way. I have an older brother."

"Oh." I was immediately curious. I liked the feelings I got when I was friends with a girl with an older brother.

"Y'all on vacation?" Charlotte Ann asked.

"No. We're moving here. We just rented a house."

My mom appeared then, and I was not about to ask any questions about Charlotte Ann's brother, even ones that sounded as if I weren't really asking about him.

"Isn't it a beautiful evening?" Mom asked.

"Yes, ma'am," Charlotte Ann responded.

It *was* a beautiful evening. The friendly breeze was as warm and soft as the night before, and very clean. I could see the tops of palm trees near the road, swaying ever so slightly. Cars hummed, the sound muffled by the breeze and the crickets and the glimmering aquamarine water lapping the sides of the pool.

"The Texas sky is just as the song says, isn't it, Meredith?" My mom sighed as she looked up. I was relieved she didn't start singing about the stars at night being big and bright.

"I've never known anything else," Charlotte Ann said. "I like the name Meredith."

"I like it too," Mom said. She took off her flannel shirt and revealed to the world that she took swimming seriously.

"Oh, Mom."

"Still don't like my navy tank suit, huh?"

"Nope."

"Why don't you go put on your suit and swim with me and . . ."

"Charlotte Ann," I said. "She lives here."

"Nice to meet you." My mother nodded at Charlotte Ann and then tested the water with a toe.

"Where's your house?" Charlotte Ann asked.

"I don't know." I shrugged my shoulders.

"About a mile from here." Mom put on her swimming cap and goggles and dove gracefully into the water. The lights from the pool made the splashy drops of water look like sparkling liquid diamonds. It was sort of like a fountain—rich and smooth and beautiful all at once. Delicate too. I wondered if my grandmother thought I had something as lovely as that in me. If she did, then she did see me as very special.

"I thought she was your sister," Charlotte Ann whispered.

"No. I have a sister, though." Then I realized I was going to have to explain Tina to a whole bunch of new people.

"Do you want to go to The Rainbow Pavilion?" Charlotte Ann asked. "It's an ice cream parlor and candy store down the road a couple blocks."

"Sure." The idea was okay with Mom so long as we were careful about traffic.

"I have to change." Charlotte Ann carefully tiptoed on bare feet across gravel and grass full of burrs, and I followed. By the orange bug lights in front of the motel units, I searched for black widows and scorpions and rattlesnakes, all of which were supposed to be living right here in Texas.

The motel units were white stucco with dark tile roofs. A border of brightly colored tiles, arranged to show market scenes in Mexico, trimmed the bottom of each picture window. A television glowed through gold drapes in almost every unit.

Suddenly I saw the mobile home, long and bleak looking, sitting in an empty field full of swaying brush and sturdy cactus and scraggly trees that I had already learned were called mesquite. I had never been in a mobile home and I was curious.

Charlotte Ann pulled open the screen door, battered and tightly sprung so it banged against my calf. That hurt quite a bit but I was utterly silent. I would have had to shout anyway to be heard over the roaring laughter on the television.

"My grandma. It's her favorite show." Charlotte Ann nodded at a woman dressed in baggy plaid pants and a man's striped shirt. She was sitting on a dark green couch covered with clothes, ironing on top of a towel spread across the coffee table and watching a game show. She had long white hair done in pigtails. Hot pink bows were tied in them. That was the nice thing about being old, I thought. You can do and wear whatever you want, whenever you want. Old people don't treat life like a fashion show.

The woman nodded at us and smiled. "If I was on the show tonight, Charlotte Ann, I'd have made a fortune."

"Well just make sure when you do that you don't pick out any more tacky furniture for your prize. We have plenty already."

"The problem with you, Charlotte Ann, is that you don't appreciate." There was a burst of applause from the television, and Charlotte Ann's grandma turned all her attention to the show.

"My father furnished this place with old motel-room furniture," Charlotte Ann whispered so only I could hear. "How can I appreciate that? Once we're out of debt, Mom wants to get a house and furnish it in style."

We then walked down a narrow, dark hall, plastic wood all around. I kept expecting to feel the floor sway like on a boat.

I didn't directly watch Charlotte Ann dress, but I got a good look at her because she was reflected in a mirror that hung lopsided on her closet door. She was awfully thin and not grown much. After she combed her short red hair, she crinkled and smushed it with her hands and I could see she had an awful lot of natural curl. "Nice room," I said. Her room was very neat except for the lopsided mirror, and she had a lovely pink satin bedspread.

Charlotte Ann turned toward me. In the light I thought she looked like an old lady the way her forehead puckered and her eyes squinted, as if her glasses didn't fit or work quite right. She looked worried. It wasn't till much later that I began to understand why she looked as she did. It wasn't just because her parents were divorced and her father had left them with a bunch of money problems.

"I'm glad you like my room. Pink's my favorite color."

"I don't really have one." I lied. I don't know why. Maybe I didn't want Charlotte Ann to know too much about me or think I was a lot like her. Pink's my favorite color, too. And I was confused. I pretty much liked the first Texan I'd met and that was something I hadn't expected.

I took out my notebook first thing when I got back to the motel and wrote a quick note.

August 28

Dear Grandma,

I just met a girl named Charlotte Ann. I think she might become a friend. She took me to an ice cream and candy shop called The Rainbow Pavilion. The place reminded me of you. They sell divinity there, the old-fashioned kind, but not nearly as good as what you made.

Do you miss me as much as I miss you? Is there anything in heaven that reminds you of me?

Well, I've got to go to bed. I hope Mom doesn't notice I didn't brush my teeth. I'd like to fall asleep with the taste of divinity in my mouth.

'Nite for now,
Meredith

P.S.   For your sake I hope they have chocolate and marshmallow sauce and divinity candy in heaven. Do they?

Chapter · 3 ·

Dad took us and the U-haul trailer with our beds and some other furniture to our new home and then left. He had to be at a ten o'clock meeting at his office. He said it wasn't going to be a real work day and he'd be back soon. We'd all heard that before.

"Let's take a tour and see what needs cleaning," Mom signed and spoke. "We can buy this house if we want, so let me know what you think."

I realized then that Adam wasn't with us. I found him sitting on the patio.

"Look, Mama Cat." He pointed a finger, which was beginning to look different from the pudgy little baby fingers I loved to hold, at a tiny bug crawling along the smooth, cool cement. I touched one of the dull black creatures, no bigger than my little fingernail, and it rolled into a ball the size of a small pea. I squatted and watched while at least a hundred paper-thin legs began to wiggle and the oblong body unfolded. With a superb sense of timing and rhythm, the roly-poly righted itself. There were faint lines like joints along its back, and I wondered what sort of sound

17

it made when stepped on. A crunch of some kind. It was so frag-
ile I could have smashed it, or one of its several brothers or sisters
who were also meandering around the patio, with a single finger.

Tina joined us. She spelled out "doodle bugs" and we made
up a sign for them, making a "d," the thumb touching the last three
fingers with the index finger held erect, and slowly rolled it up into
a loose fist. Pretty soon we were shooting them around the patio
like marbles. No one got hurt until Adam began to crawl after
them and crunched two with his right knee. He got very upset,
and Tina and I felt bad. I wasn't sure if I felt worse for Adam
or the doodle bugs. We tiptoed around them when Mom came
outside to see what was keeping us.

"These are banana trees." She pointed at some shiny, big-
leaved stalks along one side of the patio. "And bamboo." We had
a whole curtain of bamboo along the west side, a perfect screen
from the hot afternoon sun.

Tina asked if we would get bananas, moving her fingers excit-
edly.

"I asked Mrs. Nowlin, the landlady. She said no. I guess it's
not warm enough."

We walked around to the front of the house, which was white
brick with dark brown trim. A large mesquite tree sat in the middle of the front yard and there were two short palm trees at the
curb standing guard on either side of the front walk.

The house had a courtyard in front, a private sort of patio full
of pretty white pebbles, but also tall, flourishing weeds. "I'd like
to fix this up," Mom said, "with some pretty chairs and gerani-
ums in pots. It looks awfully like a desert right now, but Mrs.
Nowlin says the west side of the house becomes a field of bluebonnets in the spring. You can't pick them."

"Is there something wrong with them?" I asked. I was thinking
of Adam. He was good now about not putting anything and

everything into his mouth, but not perfect. And he was always finding the oddest, and usually most dangerous, things.

"N-no. Sta' fl'er," Tina signed and spoke. She was telling me that the bluebonnet is the state flower. I think she speaks real well for never having heard. Most of the time Tina's voice is silent, her fingers dancing the words she can't speak.

"And there are climbing roses on the fence and gardenia bushes right below the bedroom windows."

"Weed?" Tina asked Mom.

"Good idea." Mom flicked her forehead. Sometimes I think sign language, and the way it refers to parts of the body, makes a lot more sense than the spoken word.

Soon we were all digging and pulling. The sun rose higher. Even though I was in the shade of the courtyard, I was sure I would soon die of heatstroke. Mom had long since taken off the flannel shirt she wore inside the house, which was air conditioned and chilly. Mom cooked in a flannel shirt, cleaned house in a flannel shirt, and had kept a flannel shirt at her office. Sometimes she slept in a flannel shirt. She said the shirt was a carryover from her college days when they called people like her "flower children." I was glad she'd passed through that phase okay and that most of the time she looked pretty fashionable.

The sun was directly overhead now and the courtyard became blindingly white. There was not a weed in sight, thanks to our hard work.

"I wonder what's keeping Mac?" Mom looked at her watch. I could tell by my stomach that it was long past lunchtime.

We had no food, no phone, no idea of how long a walk it would be to find food, so we kept working. We unloaded mattresses from our trailer. Then it hit me that there were only three bedrooms. In Chicago there had been four bedrooms, and I'd had my own room.

"But this seems like we're going backward. Like into a depression," I pointed out. "Not progress. I had my own room in Chicago." Partly I liked the idea of sharing a room and being closer to Tina, but mostly I wanted privacy. Privacy for my letters. Privacy for my feelings. Probably privacy for my body too.

I plopped down on the mattress we had just let fall on the floor in Tina's and my bedroom. There were two built-in desks along one wall with bookshelves and plenty of drawers. I guess the home builder figured the room was big enough for two and I wasn't quite sure how I was going to argue my case. Mom and Tina sat down on the mattress, sort of squatting, their feet securely planted on the plush gold-brown carpet.

"Tina won't be here most of the time," Mom began.

"I don't understand. What are you keeping from me now?" I stood up. I didn't bother to sign, but I knew Tina understood my surprise.

Suddenly Adam screamed. Mom ran out of the room. I figured he had caught his fingers in the sliding glass door again and I explained that to Tina. Then I began to question her about what was happening. "What did Mom mean you won't be here?"

"Going to school for deaf."

"What?"

"Not going to hearing school."

"Didn't you like the public school in Chicago?"

"Not much deaf." Tina had been going to a regular school for as long as I could remember, though I once heard Mom say Tina had gone to a special school when she was little. The public school system decided to hire interpreters for the deaf in regular classes. They called it mainstreaming and I figured because it was such a neat name it had to be a good idea. This past year, though, Tina had been the only deaf person in most of her classes.

"Maybe it would be different here. Don't they mainstream here too?" I asked.

"Maybe. I don't know. I'm going to The Texas School for the Deaf in Austin."

"Where?"

"Austin."

"Not even in San Antonio?"

"No."

"Far away?"

"About one hundred miles."

"You can't go."

"I want to go. Yes."

"No one told me. You can't leave us."

"I'm going to school with other deaf. I'm not leaving you. It's because we moved. That's all. It's something I decided to do. I'm not leaving you."

"Yes you are," I rapidly signed and spoke back. "Why?"

"Why not?"

"Because this is home. You belong at home. You're the oldest, but you're not even sixteen yet." My hands were flying as I signed. The only teenagers I'd heard about who left home had run away.

Then I learned, for the first time, that Tina felt alone, alone at school, maybe even alone with us, though she didn't say that. She was lonely and wanted to go to high school with other deaf boys and girls, to date and party and have fun. She didn't want to be so afraid all the time, on edge, with only hearing people around. I understood what she was telling me but it didn't help.

"Going to see if Adam's okay," she signed.

She left the room and I sat down hard on the mattress, hoping to quiet my confusion. I was losing my sister; things for my family were going to be even more changed around than I'd expected.

Everything in my life kept changing, and I was beginning to feel I couldn't count on anything or anyone. The way I'd been feeling lately, sort of like a roller coaster, was enough to make me feel I couldn't even count on myself.

I needed privacy to sort all this out. I could hear Tina and Mom in the bathroom, washing Adam's smashed finger. He was going to be okay, but I wasn't.

I walked down the hall and out the front door. And then I started to run. It was funny to be running, because I didn't know where I was going.

I sailed across the yard and up the block. It was funny, but suddenly *I* was the one running away from home.

I discovered a park a few blocks from our house and there I slowed to a walk. It was a park with tennis courts and a swimming pool. I thought of Charlotte Ann and missed her.

There were banana trees all along the fence and a clump of palm trees in a rock garden near the parking lot. I sat down to rest and think.

It didn't seem right that Tina should leave home because she wanted deaf people more than us. I felt abandoned and worried too. We were her family and supposed to protect her. What if she got into some kind of jam where she needed hearing people with her, where she needed us?

It scared me to think of being without Tina. Lots of times I felt forgotten in my family. Both Tina and Adam needed and got special attention, and I was left alone. Maybe I'd get into more trouble after she left. Or maybe I wouldn't get any more attention than I already got. Maybe I didn't get special attention from Mom and Dad because I wasn't special to them. Maybe I wasn't even likable. Lately I hadn't even liked myself.

I thought how much easier things seemed when Grandma was alive. I cried for a while, until I started feeling too lonely to keep crying. It would have been great, right then, if someone from my family had come looking for me. But I wasn't sure anyone had even noticed I was gone.

I headed home, not feeling any better. As I came down the street, Dad drove into the driveway, coming from the opposite direction. He waved when he got out of the car and I half waved back.

"What's wrong, sport?" he called out. It was a hot day and he had taken off his tie and jacket.

"Nothing."

He walked down the driveway toward me. "Looks like something to me."

"I just found out about Tina going away to school, that's all."

"Hmmm. And you weren't happy, I guess."

"Why should I be?"

"Oh, I don't know. Sometimes she complicates things. You'll have a room to yourself."

"Well, that's not bad news."

"You know," he said, "I think Tina's only beginning to understand that her life is different from ours. Meeting Jessica Porter last Christmas helped her see that she's going to be deaf all her life." Jessica Porter was a deaf woman in Chicago. She married a man Dad worked with and we went to their wedding. It was a beautiful wedding, with trumpets and Christmas caroling, the deaf singing with their hands and arms. After that Tina met some other deaf adults because of Jessica.

"But why does she have to go away?"

"It's not that she *has* to do anything, Meredith. She *wants* to go away. She has a community she belongs to that's different from us and is very important to her." Dad put his arm around me. His shirt was white and clean and starchy and felt wonderfully fresh against my face.

"I guess I wish I was in Tina's community too." I was starting to cry again. I wished even more that Grandma was still part of my community, but I didn't bring that up.

He squeezed me closer to him. "We'll always be part of Tina's community. She's growing up now. Just like you are. We'll all have to grow up a little bit with her. Don't think of it as goodbye for good."

"Like Grandma?"

"Right. Tina will be back on some weekends and probably all summer."

"Maybe she'll get a boyfriend."

Dad laughed. "Maybe she will. We'll have to get a teletypewriter attached to the phone then." A teletypewriter's a machine so deaf people can communicate by phone.

"That would be fun."

"So it's fun you want?"

"Sure."

He started walking, heading us both in the direction of the house. "Well, I was thinking maybe you guys would like to see the Alamo."

"The real Alamo?"

"The real thing. And how about some lunch? Well, I guess it's more like supper. I'm sorry."

"That's okay. Let's go eat. I'm starved." Dad kept his arm around me all the way into the house. He even offered to teach me tennis at the park when I told him about the courts. It felt real cozy. Tina was all upset because she hadn't been able to find me, and she gave me a big hug.

At first we drove through busy downtown streets and I assumed we were going to do some shopping or eat before going out to the country to see the Alamo. But then there it was, right in the middle of all the downtown buildings, pale yellow rocks reflecting the sun, bright as I expected heaven to be, not at all reminding me of the bloody battles I'd read about where heroes like Jim Bowie and Davy Crockett and William Travis lost their lives fighting for Texas's independence against Santa Ana and the Mexican army. Everyone who fought with them, about two hundred men, died too. With all the glory from that battle, it was hard to remember that the Alamo was really a simple Franciscan mission.

The Alamo was no more than a story high, and gave me the feeling that with the right equipment it could be scraped from the ground and hung from my charm bracelet, but it had a stateliness that was special. Mesquite trees and palms beckoned with green arms toward the large, rough wooden gates and I went inside very eagerly. There I found oil paintings of the Alamo heroes and weapons, life-size scenes dramatizing the battle and historic papers.

Later, after we ate, we walked along the San Antonio River. Walking bridges arched the river, and palms and banana trees were everywhere. The air was moist and sweet. Big passenger boats glided through the water, and individual paddle boats splashed here and there. On one large barge, a group of people ate dinner at a long candlelit table covered with a fresh white cloth. Twilight came, and women with raven black hair and fancy Spanish dresses rushed by to the sound of Mexican guitars floating from riverside cafés.

When we got home I managed finally to write my first long, Texas letter to Grandma.

August 29

Dear Grandma,

This was some day. I worked hard, thought hard, and cried hard. I don't like to cry in front of people anymore. I need privacy for that. Besides, no one can comfort me like you did.

So now I want to thank you for how you did that for me. And for letting me see you cry a couple times. Do you remember how I brought you apple juice when your friend Elsie Schmidt moved into the old folks home? You said I was a real comfort. That was real important to me. It made me feel good about myself. Do you think a person can cry too much? I wonder about that because I never saw Dad cry when you died.

What did you think of the Alamo? My favorite part was all those chubby goldfish they have swimming in the stream and hiding under the bridge. I can't wait to go back and bring them some food.

The river walk was exciting. I told Mom I want to take flamenco-dancing lessons. I'd like a tight dress with a slit and ruffles at the bottom. She said we'd see.

All these changes are a little scary. Was death another change, only scarier? Did dying make you cry, or were you happy?

Well, I'm tired. Tina should be almost done with her bath. We share a double bed now. Did you know that? I wonder if she'll let me hold her hand while we fall asleep. I just might like to do that.

Love ya,
Meredith

Chapter • 4 •

The movers didn't come the next day with our furniture, so I registered for school. And they didn't come the next day either. Mom said that sometimes they don't arrive as scheduled. I wish people were as accepting when I didn't live up to expectations.

Mom was making things pretty and cozy for us without all our furniture. She seemed to want to do some fun things before she went back to work as a lawyer, and she talked about taking a cooking class. I like it when adults have fun. And I like it when my mom stays home.

My father is not a playful man. In San Antonio he was beginning to sit outside on the patio to read the newspaper. That's about as playful as he's ever gotten. It was a start though. Maybe he would keep his promise about teaching me tennis.

Early the first Saturday morning in our new house, we ate breakfast on the patio. There was a breeze, though Dad said it was going to be a scorcher. Mom set down the bowl of scrambled eggs she'd just fixed and spoke and signed, "I called Honeysuckle Farms. It's a riding stable and they're starting a class for beginners this morning at ten. Do you want to take lessons, Meredith?"

27

"Sure," I answered. "But I don't have the right clothes." Dad teased me by pretending to choke on a piece of bacon. I just stared him down.

"I don't think you need anything special to start," Mom said. She was always saying things like that in a very practical sort of way.

"Are you going to go?" I asked Mom.

"Sure."

"Me too," Adam chimed in.

"I thought maybe you could get on a horse with me, Adam. Tina, you want to go?"

"Okay."

"They don't have a way to teach deaf, Tina," Mom explained. "Meredith can take a beginner's class and maybe you, me, and Adam can work something out with an instructor. We'll see."

"Dad could take a class with me," I suggested.

"But I don't have a single thing to wear."

"Oh, *Dad*."

Just then this long truck pulled up to the curb. The movers had arrived. Mom and Dad looked at each other. I thought for sure my riding adventure was ruined.

"You guys go," Dad said. "I'll do the best I can with the movers."

"Oh, Mac, thanks." Mom looked as if she were going to kiss him, and I was very glad when she did. I really do like to see my mother get excited and have fun. When she acts silly and playful, I feel happier. It makes growing up look like a better deal.

We gathered up the dishes and Dad went to meet the truck drivers.

"Meredith, do you want to wear my boots?" Mom and I wear the same size shoes. She had gotten a pair of cowboy boots on

Maxwell Street in Chicago, to wear with skirts. They were so nice she'd worn them to court.

"That's okay," I said. I absolutely hate the expression "that's okay" because I never know what the person means by it and I wasn't sure what I meant.

"Oh, go ahead."

"But I might ruin them or something."

"I doubt it. Besides, I don't think I could stand it if you embarrassed us by not having the right clothes."

"Oh, Mom." I don't think they understand about clothes. Looking good and fitting in had seemed more important than anything in Chicago, and I couldn't imagine that Texas, with all its supposedly gorgeous people, would be any different. I threw on my best jeans, my mom's boots, and the cowboy shirt I'd gotten for a square-dancing number in sixth grade where I had to play a boy.

"I think those go over there," Dad was saying to the movers as we went out the back door. He didn't sound very sure of himself, but I had all the confidence in the world in him.

We drove past the junior high where I would start school in a few days and then into rolling hills full of stubbly sagebrush, rugged mesquite, and proud cactus. I pictured myself racing across the range to rescue a baby calf from a coyote on my dream horse, Ginger. The car turned down a dirt road. Ahead was an aqua metal building, not at all like the honeysuckle-covered old barn I had pictured. An awfully tall horse out in the pasture watched me arrive. He made feel a little bit chicken.

Mom pulled the car up to the building alongside at least ten empty cars. "Isn't this great?" she got out of the car, stretched her arms, and took in a deep breath. Adam imitated her. A blue sedan pulled in beside us and I glanced quickly at the back seat. Two sparkling blonde girls normally would prod my competitive spirit and make me hop right out of the car, but I was so scared that I didn't.

Mom poked her head back in the car. "Are you okay, Meredith?"

"I feel a little sick."

"To your stomach?"

"Yeah."

"You'll be riding outside in the fresh air. It won't smell bad."

"It's not the smell."

"What is it?"

"I guess I'm scared."

Mom sat down sideways, rested her arms on the back of the front seat, and looked at me. "They'll help you get up on the horse, Meredith. You don't have to do everything perfectly today. Nobody expects that. Once you're up you'll be fine. And they'll help you get down. They'll help you with anything that's a problem."

"There's not much room up there."

"There's a saddle and reins . . ."

"And it's a long way down."

"It's not any different from the elephant ride at the Lincoln Park Zoo."

"That was awful."

"But you had fun."

"After it was over."

"So, after this is over, you'll feel good. It's good to do the things you fear. You learn a lot about yourself that way."

A brilliant cherry-red pickup truck pulled up and two boys hopped down. They were both wearing plaid shirts, vests, jeans, and cowboy boots. The one with curly reddish-brown hair, almost flamelike, stooped and talked to Adam, who was watching some insect. I liked how he looked and how friendly he acted. He seemed about my age. The other boy was older.

"Okay," I said as I reached for the door handle. I stretched full-chested as the redheaded boy stood up and began to walk by me. I wanted him to notice me.

"Hey, Scotty." One of the blonde girls caught his attention right away.

"Amabel," he shouted. "Did ya know m' brother's teaching intermediate?"

"Amabel?" I muttered to myself. I couldn't tell if Scotty had noticed me, but I doubted it. I followed Mom, who had gathered up a dusty Adam, and Tina into the barn.

The stalls were wood, and they lined the full length of one wall and part of the other. The building was enormous and dimly lit.

Some stalls were empty except for their thick sawdust and wood-chip carpeting. In others, horses stood staring into space, held back only by a chain. Each stall had a name and what looked like medical instructions on a chalkboard. Izzy got so much feed and some pill. And there was Sebastian and Hard Rain and Moonraker. I was thinking about what I would name my horse. Ginger was too ordinary. Maybe Pink Cloud.

"A dancing horse, Mama Cat," Adam called out to me. Where he was pointing I could see hooves moving in the stall. Hoping no one outside my family had heard him call me Mama Cat, I hurried ahead, past a long wagon attached to a small orange tractor. I didn't want to miss a dancing horse. Maybe I'd call my horse Pink Prancer.

Suddenly I was sprayed with sawdust flung from a stall. I swung out my arms to protect my head. My mouth sputtered and spit. For one moment I gagged, unable to breathe. I shook my hair, spinning off sawdust and little blackish-brown particles. I looked down and saw one of these particles stuck to my belly, resting on my belt. I picked it up. It was horse poop. I thought I might throw up.

"I'm sorry," said a young woman carrying a pitchfork. "I didn't think anyone was walking along this side since I have it blocked with the truck." She started to brush me off. "I'm cleaning out all the stalls."

"It's okay," I said with a voice that didn't seem to be mine. I felt completely off guard and a little wounded.

Someone started to laugh and I turned, suddenly face to face with Scotty. He was pulling bits and pieces of sawdust and I knew not what else from my hair.

"It isn't funny." I felt he was laughing at me and no matter what I thought about *his* hair, how it looked like flames dancing in the sun, I instantly disliked him.

"I'm sorry. I'm not laughing at you."

"Well, you're not laughing *with* me. Do you see *me* laughing?" I was annoyed. "Do I smell?" I asked the girl who had spattered me.

"It's hard to tell," she answered.

"It *was* funny," Scotty said. "I was watchin' you lookin' so curious in each of the stalls, checking out everythin', and then wham." He snickered. "I coulda died laughin'."

"Then drop dead!" I knew I didn't really wish death on anyone, not a single human being. I softened, but not enough to laugh. "I'm sorry. I don't mean that."

"It's okay. You should get a hat." He gave me a big smile.

I nodded and walked away. I tried to look straight ahead, but out of the corners of my eyes I strained to get an idea of who had seen what. The two shimmering blondes were talking about me. I could tell that, just as I could tell my mom and Tina had been laughing.

"Looks like you were caught in quite a shower, honey," my mother said without cracking a smile. She picked off the pieces that had stuck more forcefully. When she pinched her nose shut I started to laugh. Then I saw that Scotty was still watching me. He smiled again and this time I smiled back, feeling somehow helpless to do anything else. I grew warm inside, excited that he had been watching me all that time I had been looking at the horses and I hadn't even done anything special. I hadn't even *tried* to get him to notice me.

But I didn't want Scotty, who stood at the railing, or anyone in my class, to laugh at me ever again. In spite of my shaking inside, I got right on my horse, Hoover Jean. The teacher told me she was named after the vacuum cleaner. And I didn't scream bloody murder when she started to trot, and I felt sure I was going to bounce right off her rump.

At the end of the class I signed up for the entire ten-week session, but not exactly to learn to ride.

September 3

Dear Grandma,

I had the most exciting day. I took my first horseback-riding lesson. And guess what? I signed up for more.

I was a little scared. We're not learning Western. It's English riding and so there's no horn on the saddle like in the movies. When we started to trot a little I would have liked one, but I grabbed the mane instead. We're not supposed to use cowboy words like "corral" either. I really didn't think there would be so many rules to riding a horse. It makes it a lot less fun. At least so far. Maybe that's just the way with lessons.

The riding teacher, Sarah Bess, has a wide rear end. Do you think that comes from riding?

I met a boy named Scotty. I don't know what to think of him. I bet he thinks I'm a real nerd. I bet he thinks Mama Cat is a nerdo nickname. What do you think?

Personally, I can't wait to see him again. I'll keep you informed.

Nice talking to you,
Mama Cat Meredith

Chapter · 5 ·

September 5

Dear Grandma,

Yesterday we took Tina up to Austin to school. That meant I couldn't go to visit Charlotte Ann like I wanted. I sure miss her. As soon as things get a little less busy around here, Mom says I can have her over for the night. I think she'd like to see my house.

I've been thinking a lot about death. I think I dreamed about it last night. Death came as a man all in black. A softer and bigger man than an ordinary man, very friendly and handsome and powerful. I wasn't afraid at all. He was like a good friend I've known for a long time. I was glad to see him. He almost seemed like a part of me, but how could he have been part of me? Anyway, it was only a dream.

I adjusted okay to Tina going. I think. Her school is like a camp and she lives in a cottage with about thirty other girls. I was a little frightened at first, being around so many deaf people, but I think I understand Tina a little bit better. I think she'll have fun. Maybe she'll have more fun than with us. Everyone there was real excited to meet her. I sure hope she writes me.

Well, I'm going to go watch TV and try to forget I go to a new school tomorrow. Wish me luck. Or pray for me!

Love, Meredith

P.S. What's it like to be in heaven? Does it give you any better idea of what God's like? Does He really see the big picture?

I had just gotten comfortable when the phone rang. It turned out to be my first phone call in Texas.

"Hi. Is this Meredith?"

"Yup."

"It's me, Charlotte Ann."

"Charlotte Ann!" I was surprised but not surprised. She'd been on my mind a lot the past week. "How'd you get our number?"

"Remember I told you my mother had a second job? She's a part-time secretary at Crockett Junior High. She saw your name on a registration card and wrote down your phone number and address. I had her drive me by your house yesterday, but you weren't there."

"No. We were out for a while." I felt uncomfortable about explaining Tina over the phone so I didn't.

"It's a nice house."

"We just rent."

"It's still nice." She paused. "Guess what?"

"What?"

"Come on, guess. It's no fun if you don't guess."

I've never thought having to guess made a surprise any more fun. I'm one of those people who wants to know the good stuff right away. But the bold determination in Charlotte Ann's voice was a challenge.

"Um . . . your mom knows my class schedule." I wasn't going

to know my schedule until I went to the principal's office the next morning to get my homeroom assignment.

"That too. More."

"They couldn't squeeze me into a gym class."

"No. But you're getting warm. We're in the same phys-ed class."

"You're kidding!" I whooped. "So you go to Crockett too?"

"Yeah. We're just inside the district. It's pretty big the other direction—out to some ranches."

"We'll have cowboys?"

"Sure. You and I have Texas History, Science and Advanced English together, too, but we have different math teachers."

"So how much of the day are we together?"

"Mom's trying to get us into the same Spanish class. If she does we'll be together all morning and the last two periods in the afternoon. We can go from gym to lunch together if you want."

"Oh, Charlotte Ann. I'd love to. Tell your mother thanks. I hope she swings Spanish."

"Me too."

"Does your brother go there too?"

"Yup. He's in ninth grade."

"That must be nice." Maybe now I would get my chance to meet her older brother.

"I guess. It's my first year there. I'm not very sure Pete's ever been good to have around. Are you going to take the bus?"

"I don't know. I don't think I'll take it tomorrow. Maybe after that." I was starting to get nervous again, thinking about going to a new place. A new place for seventh grade.

"If you take the bus I will too. I can go with my mom, though, if I want."

We chatted for a long time. It seemed exciting to be going to junior high after all, and I felt I would have a lot of fun with Charlotte Ann.

I fell asleep thinking about God. Not a whole lot, just a little. I thought about heaven and earth and started to imagine that maybe someday I would live in a mobile home, a pink mobile home with my horse, Pink Prancer, in a nearby pasture. I wondered if God would think that too silly a way to live.

It must have been ninety degrees by seven-thirty the next morning when I walked out onto the patio.

"Meredith. You can't wear blue jeans. Not in this heat." Mom set down the newspaper, which meant she was ready to spend some time discussing what I was going to wear.

"Charlotte Ann says this is what everyone wears."

"But it's going to be boiling hot."

I wasn't about to tell her I felt hotter in the two minutes I'd been outside than I'd ever been. It was even hotter than last year's Fourth of July when I wore my new designer jeans at Lake Michigan and the sweat stained my crotch so that Ed Gleason thought I'd peed my pants and told everyone.

"Blue jeans just look hot," I said in my most pleasant, easygoing conversational tone. "You know how dark colors are."

Mom put on her "let's-go-investigate-your-closet" look and I knew that nothing could be done. "How about that flowered skirt?" she suggested.

"But Mom."

"Go."

Inside, I picked up my lunch from the kitchen counter and ran to my room. My sandwich and apple went inside the pockets of my winter coat hanging in the closet. I stuffed my jeans into the empty sack. I had a plan to please my mother and to fit in. It was getting harder and harder to do both. If I had to choose, I'd choose to fit in.

"Much better," Mom said when she saw me in my skirt. And then she and Adam and I got in the car and off we went.

I was awfully nervous, and Mom could tell. "Try to think of Charlotte Ann," she suggested. "Maybe some of those kids in your riding class go to Crockett. Like that redheaded boy. You'll have fun."

Charlotte Ann was in my homeroom. I learned later that her last name's Kincaid and that the K's and Mc's went together. She waved at me as Mr. Clements, the principal, brought me into the class. He sure made a production of it, and I got too embarrassed to see clearly and check for dresses. I was glad when I could take a seat like a normal kid. I wanted to get my skirt under the desk as soon as possible, in case it really was the only one.

Once seated I hurriedly looked around. There were a few Southern belles, prettier even than Jeannie back in Chicago, and I thought it would do her good to come for a visit. To my great relief Charlotte Ann had not changed, at least not in appearance.

Once I had a chance to check out the scene, I discovered all the girls were in slacks and jeans except me. Somehow I sensed they knew my mother had made me wear a dress and they wouldn't hold it against me.

The homeroom teacher, Ms. Stetson, repeated some of what I had missed, but I missed it then too. I had never moved before, so I had never been new to a school except first grade. I guess I felt a little like I was starting first grade, a little shaken. And I had never had to change classes every fifty minutes either. At one point, while Ms. Stetson was talking about being in the hall between classes and how the rooms were numbered, I got a sort of teary-eyed wish for my mom. Boy, did I feel like a baby then. But when I remembered Mom had not let me wear jeans, I figured she would be no help. Slowly, I started to pay attention.

"I like your skirt," Charlotte Ann said as soon as the bell rang.

"Thanks. I'm freezing though. I have my jeans in here if I have time to change now." I squeezed my sack to my chest, hoping to keep myself warm. The school was so air conditioned it felt like the North Pole.

"I'm not sure we have time for you to change 'cause I've never been to this school before either, but there's a restroom at the end of the hall. My mother warned me about the cold. I have a sweater in my locker if you need it."

"Thanks."

We pushed our way through the crowded hall toward the restroom. And then, for a brief second, I saw him. Scotty, that is. Mom had good intuition and she could be right sometimes.

I changed clothes quickly, but Charlotte Ann and I were still late for Texas History. It didn't matter much, since others were late too. One girl got completely lost and was ten minutes late. All of us seventh graders were new to Crockett, so in some ways I was not that different. And Charlotte Ann took very good care of me.

In gym class I met Claire Ellen. Claire Ellen definitely was a Southern belle, a girl who in my eyes had all the makings of another Cheryl Tiegs. It was hard to imagine her as twelve. Girls and boys didn't have gym together, but we had classes going on at the same time in the same gym. That was when I saw Scotty again. This time I saw he had thin legs with the faintest glow of reddish-brown hair.

"Claire Ellen has the hots for him," Charlotte Ann whispered as the girls' class formed a circle on the gym floor and the boys filed out the door and began jogging toward the outdoor track.

"The what?"

"The hots. Don't you know . . ."

"Of course I know. Who are you talking about?"

"Claire Ellen and that guy you were staring at—Scotty."

I was embarrassed. "What guy?" I asked with as much inno-
cence as my voice could muster.

She nudged me. "You know." Roll was being called and she
whispered, "His name's Scotty. Scott Dumont. Cute, huh?"

I didn't answer her, but I couldn't have agreed more.

Tina came home that weekend. She was having a great time at
school, but she missed us. We all went back to Honeysuckle
Farms on Saturday, but I didn't see Scotty. I almost fell off my
horse looking for him. He hadn't seen me at school as far as I
could tell, but I wanted to hear him say, "Hi, haven't I seen you
playing volleyball in gym? Fantastic serve." Or something close
to that. Actually, anything would do.

"Who you looking for?" Tina signed.

"No one."

"I can tell." She smirked, and when I turned away she giggled
in her loud way. She touched my shoulder to turn me around so
she could sign. "That boy with the red hair."

I shook my head "no."

"Sweet on him?"

"I don't think so. He goes to my school."

"Good." And then she crossed her arms and laid them against
her chest, the sign for love. I sincerely doubted it was love, but I
sure had a feeling for him.

After my riding lesson, Mom dropped me off at Charlotte
Ann's for lunch and a swim. Charlotte Ann met Tina and Adam
for the first time and we all met her older brother Pete, who was
carrying a load of dirty towels toward their mobile home when we
pulled up. At first I thought I wasn't interested in Pete, but I was
wrong. As soon as Charlotte Ann and I got to the pool I began
asking questions about him. I was not surprised to find out that
he had been a star basketball player in eighth grade and now, in

the ninth, was on the A team for the school. And he was captain of the school's tennis team.

"Does he give tennis lessons?" I asked.

Charlotte Ann laughed. "He's not that good. You know who's probably better? Scotty Dumont. Maybe you could get him . . ."

I dove under water to cool the blush I felt start to flood my face. The idea of becoming a tennis star raced through my mind.

"Come back here," Charlotte Ann called out. "I have some questions for you."

"Like what?"

"How'd your sister get like that?"

"What do you mean?"

"I mean, she can't hear or talk, right? She makes all those weird movements with her hands. She sounds funny."

"I never think about her *getting* some way. She's been like that ever since I've known her."

"Was she born like that?"

"Yeah. Just like you were born the way you are. You can't help yourself either." Those words just rattled off my tongue.

"So what's she going to do to take care of herself? You have to hear to be able to do anything."

"You must be kidding. If I didn't hear you I'd be a lot better off." Charlotte Ann splashed me. "Tina wants to be an actress," I admitted.

Charlotte Ann started to laugh. "Who would pay for that? She sounds retarded when she tries to talk."

I floated away on my back. I really liked Charlotte Ann, bold determination and all, but I sure didn't like what she was saying. "And she hears voices," I added, just to see what kind of reaction I'd get.

"No, she doesn't."

Charlotte Ann reminded me of Adam when he was two and a

half. He said "no" to everything then and acted as if he knew better than everyone else, even when he knew the least.

"That's for me to know and you to find out. I'll let you know when she gives me the word on whether you're going to heaven."

"What?" Charlotte Ann shouted. But I breaststroked away, pretending I couldn't hear.

My mother says she doesn't believe in all the stuff people say about children like Tina being special, or specially blessed. Sometimes, though, I think it would be a blessing not to hear. Not to hear things like Charlotte Ann's big mouth, for instance.

I really don't know if Tina hears voices, like God talking to the prophets, but I imagine she very well might. Beneath all the noise of the world I think there must be a kind, sweet voice that knows and loves us very much. Sometimes I hear a voice that seems the kinder, wiser part of me. When the voice sounds deep I wonder if that's God. Grandma would know. Maybe I'll talk to Tina about all this someday, what she hears in the stillness. And maybe, someday, I'll show Charlotte Ann that the deaf can act and be paid for it.

When Pete came to the pool to swim, I let go of the differences between Charlotte Ann and me, and we became the best of friends again.

Chapter · 6 ·

Finally I got my big chance to talk to Scotty at school. I was bending over to get a drink at the little drinking fountain stuck in the wall in the gym and he came up behind me, real close to my rear end. I must have been afraid he was going to give me a good swat, because that's how I acted. I jerked forward and hit my head on the porcelain. I felt like a real nerd and didn't ever want to bring my head out to face the world, especially Scotty Dumont. But he touched my elbow, and I think he said, "Y'all okay? Sure didn't mean to push." I really didn't concentrate on the words because there was something about his voice that really—well, it almost hypnotized me. His voice seemed to send out magnetic currents that danced in my ears.

He remembered me as the girl who got sprayed by all that horse manure. I wasn't embarrassed anymore. The way he looked at me, as we talked by the water fountain, made me feel it had all been worth it anyway.

After school I wrote to Grandma.

October 9

Dear Grandma,
    I finally got to say hi at school to that boy Scotty, the one I've been so curious about. That seems to explain best what I feel

about him. I was especially curious to know if he lives on a ranch. I wanted to ask him a lot of things but my tongue didn't work so well when I was with him. I just feel something strong about him. Maybe he's a magnet in disguise.

Scotty's in eighth grade, which scared me a little. He does seem more sophisticated. I'm glad I'd practiced talking to Pete so I wasn't so nervous. He takes the riding class after mine. He's more intermediate—he even rides in rodeos where kids practice riding skills. That's western style, he said. And when he heard I'd always lived in Chicago and had never seen one, he said . . .

"Knock before you come in!" Even though it was only Adam, I leaned across my desk to hide the letter. "Mom!"

"It's Mom's jogging time. Please play Mama Cat, Baby Cat," Adam suggested as he came closer. His voice sounded about as sweet as honey and I felt myself getting stuck.

"In a minute," I said. "I'm busy."

"You writing?"

"Yes, a letter."

"To Jeannie?" Adam knew Jeannie was my best friend in Chicago.

"No."

"Why?"

"None of your business," I said harshly.

"Grandma never yelled at me when she babysat."

I felt as if the wind had been knocked out of me and I knew that in my letter I'd have to ask the secret of her kindhearted patience. "I know," I sighed.

"You think Grandma's maybe my size now?"

I knew that Adam was remembering how Grandma shrank and shrank as cancer took over her body. She looked very petite when she died. It was sad, when she could still sit and hold me, to lean back against her chest and not feel her big squishy breasts under her silky dress. Sometimes it had been more scary than sad, like I might lean and lean and find only emptiness instead of Grandma, and tumble head over heels through cold black space for all eternity.

"I think she marshmallowed when she saw God," I said.

Adam laughed. "Grandma's a marshmallow."

I couldn't talk to him about Grandma anymore. It hurt my throat. "Oh, oh," I squealed. "Where's my Baby Cat?" And Adam rushed away to hide.

I never had to look for him long, because usually he would peek out at me from his hiding place and hide his face in his hands. Then I had to call out, "Oh, Baby Cat, Baby Cat. I'm so glad to find you," and rush to him and smother him with hugs and kisses. Then we'd start again.

I got a chance to finish my letter before we ate. Mom still wasn't working, which was just fine with me. Everything seemed cozier because she was around in a relaxed sort of way. And she was becoming a real artist with Mexican food.

While I was helping with dinner dishes, Adam slid open the glass patio door and ambled in. Sometimes he's so cute and easygoing that he reminds me of those doodle bugs on the patio. He came up and leaned against my leg.

"Time?" I asked.

In the evening, while there was still light, we'd go up to the park and play "Mama Cat, Baby Cat." Lately he had wanted a "Daddy Cat" too and I wasn't sure what to do about that. As we headed out, the sun was about to set, flooding the sky with orange and rose.

At the park we had lots of room, and Adam hid behind trees and bushes, under picnic tables and grills. On about the fifth hide-and-seek I was walking through the empty tennis courts and whining, "Where's Baby Cat?" at the top of my lungs when the night lights suddenly turned twilight into brassy midday. It was like stagelights being turned on. I hoped it wasn't the cops. I turned around. It was worse than the cops. It was Scotty and Pete, Charlotte Ann's brother. Both were dressed in shiny white.

"Meredith!" I had been happy when Scotty recognized me earlier that day. Right then, when he shouted my name, I wanted to disappear.

I lowered my voice and added in a slow, drudging tone. "Hi, Scotty. Hi, Pete." Maybe they wouldn't suspect I had been the one carrying on over a lost baby cat.

"What the heck you doin', Mer?" Pete twanged. "You sound like a cat in heat. I always thought Charlotte Ann had the weirdest friends."

"What the heck *you* doing, Pete?" I asked, walking toward them and swinging my arms as if I was just out for an evening stroll.

"What's it look like?"

"Tennis."

"A genius in disguise."

"Did you lose a cat, Meredith?" I could have hugged Scotty for taking things at face value.

"Not exactly." I leaned against the cool metal post of the tennis net, not more than four feet from the two of them. I didn't think I was particularly looking at Scotty, but I could tell that, for sure, his eyes were blue. I doubted he was looking at me the way I was looking at him. Scotty started to bounce a tennis ball on his racket.

"Well, what *were* you doing? It sounded like you were calling 'baby cat.' " Pete slashed his racket through the air. I moved away from the net. They looked like two serious players.

"It's a game."

"A game? You were playing by yourself?" Pete laughed in an

evil sort of way. I could have punched him. I was getting real angry, just like old times, and I lit a fireball on Pete's head.

"Adam," I called. "Oh, Baby Cat, it's time to go."

In a minute Adam appeared at the other side of the tennis court. Part of me felt irritated at Adam because I was embarrassed, but part of me loved to see him there, in the distance, short and huggable. I scurried, bent to about half my height, across the court. "Oh, Baby Cat, Baby Cat. I am *so* glad to see you." I picked him up in a big hug and kissed his soft, cool cheek. "Baby Cat want ice cream?"

"Mama Cat. Again."

"It's getting dark."

"Okay." At three, Adam had started to become more reasonable. We held hands and I felt we sort of toddled across the court. Scotty and Pete had begun volleying.

"Your brother?" Scotty asked.

"Yup. Adam."

"Hi, Adam. You like the ponies, Adam?"

"Yeah. How'd you know about the ponies?"

"I saw you at the barn."

"Oh. I saw you too."

I realized then that Scotty was very observant and very friendly and none of it had anything to do with me. It was his style, as Dad would say. It was impossible to tell then if he really liked me. I knew, though, that I liked him a lot.

At home Adam had his ice cream and then Dad gave him a bath. Mom was sitting on the patio and I brought her a dish of sherbet. We both loved the Texas sky at night and the breeze that came all the way from the Gulf.

"Grandma would have liked it here," Mom said out of the blue. We hadn't talked about Grandma much. Mom had been in the middle of a big trial when Grandma died.

It was the sort of statement that didn't really need a response. I nodded that I agreed, and wondered how strange my mom would think me if I said I thought Grandma was here with us, in Texas, watching and having a good time.

"Meredith?"

"Yeah?"

"Do you think you're adjusting to being here? I mean, I know you weren't exactly happy with the idea of moving. Are you starting to feel settled?"

"Pretty much." Actually, at that moment I felt real uncomfortable. I wondered if Mom had found my secret letters. I felt a little guilty about writing them, and I was embarrassed to still have such strong feelings about Grandma nearly four months after she'd died. "It helps to have a friend like Charlotte Ann."

"I'm glad you met her."

I rubbed my nose and thought how Charlotte Ann had stared at me that morning after gym class. "What are you staring at?" I had finally asked.

She had answered, very truthfully and to the point, which I'd come to know as her style, "I have some good pimple scrub at home that would really help your nose. It would help till your skin gets used to how hot and humid it is here."

"I don't think so." I had felt my nose for the extra oil that had accumulated with gym class.

Now I wondered if Scotty had thought anything about my nose. Those tennis lights were awfully bright.

"I'm going to go wash my face," I announced.

"Oh," Mom said. "That sounds like a good idea."

I could tell she was stunned. She had tried to get me to wash my face at least once a day for the past year. I just couldn't remember to do it, even after Mrs. Olson, my sixth-grade teacher, had gone on and on for the benefit of the entire class about the value of deodorant, water, and soap.

" 'Night, Mom." I bent to kiss her.

" 'Night, Meredith."

I was relieved that she didn't question me anymore and let me go in peace. I didn't quite understand why, but I couldn't talk to Mom about my feelings for Grandma and everything I shared with her. Though I loved writing the letters, I knew they wouldn't be easily accepted or understood by others.

Chapter • 7•

The Mama Cat, Baby Cat episode made me resolve to learn to play tennis, especially since I evidently wasn't meant to be a horsewoman. I wanted to show Pete and Scotty I had talent for something more than screeching like a cat or being hit by horse manure. First, I needed to get in shape. I decided to try jogging.

Sunday was a beautiful day, about sixty-five degrees with a clear blue sky. Dad had cut the bamboo, flooding the patio with light from the west, and the banana-tree leaves were yellow now. But the palm trees looked no different, still green. The day had a strange sort of fall look and feel, without all the range of fall colors I was used to in Chicago. My parents and Adam had decided to surprise Tina with a visit, leaving me to do my homework. I took off toward the park as soon as they were around the corner.

Mom ran around the park six times now. That got her to five miles. I set out to run around it twice.

At first I felt as if my gym shoes contained lead weights. I even tripped on my own feet, not something new, but pretty scary at top speed. After a while, though, I had a rhythm and felt pride in my chest. Exercise felt surprisingly good. About halfway around the second time, I felt someone running with me, on the other side of the fence. I turned my head to have a look.

"You keep a pretty good pace, Meredith." It was Scotty.

I swallowed hard and kept running. I could feel my face turning cranberry red and I was sweating. I figured my heart had never pumped so fast and furiously. "Oh" was the most intelligent response I could come up with. Plus it saved breath.

"Do you jog every day?" he asked.

"No." Couldn't he tell? I must have looked like a moist beet.

"It's good exercise for your heart."

"Uh-huh." I thought I was going to die. The last part was uphill. At the stop sign I collapsed.

"What'd you do?" he asked. "We just got here. Boy, I'm real impressed."

I was dead on the grass, glad for the slippery cool green, and he was jogging in place. "I lost count," I gasped. I could feel my face explode with heat.

"You really get red."

"It runs in the family."

"Do you play tennis?"

"No."

"You'd do great on the tennis team with that kind of stamina. Come on over to the courts and watch us play. I'm here with my brother, Buff. He's captain of the high-school team."

"Okay. In a little while." As he jogged away with the greatest of graceful ease, I slithered toward some shade. My legs had hurt even before I started to run because of the little bit of horseback riding I'd done the day before. Now I wasn't sure I'd ever walk again.

I was getting a little more interested in athletics, but this freaky run-in with Scotty, whom I normally saw only in the school gym, or once in a while in the hallway, might turn me into a jock. And I was not at all sure girls were supposed to get that way.

Slowly my breath came back. I crawled to the stop sign and rested my forehead against the metal pole. Then I put one hand over the other up the post until I was standing. Sort of. I was bent at my waist, almost afraid to straighten my spine. My legs vibrated inside and gave me about as much support as barely congealed Jello. With my hands on my thighs I moved forward. The pressure of a hand on each thigh seemed to stop the shaking. Eventually I went erect, from ape to twelve-year-old. I walked slowly to cool down.

"Hey, Meredith," Scotty yelled before I was quite ready for company. "Come sit on the bench. This is Buff."

"Hi." Buff, blond and tan, nodded at me and then sent a bright yellow ball sailing across the net to Scotty, who missed it because he was watching me. My knees gave out and I crumpled to the ground. I was completely surprised.

They both ran over. Buff said I was dehydrated and Scotty ran to get their jug of water. Buff, he was even more handsome up close, picked me up in his arms, carried me over to the bench, and laid me down on it. I could feel the chill of the cement, which, together with some water, took some of the stars out of my eyes. I think I still had some for Buff, though.

Scotty and Buff returned to playing. Soon I turned from watching the sky, a peaceful baby blue, to their playing. I lay on my side with my head propped on my hand. I ran my fingers through my hair, glad that it was clean. I felt a little like a model lying there so I stayed, even after I'd recovered.

"Hey, Meredith. Want to give it a try? Buff's going to use the backboard."

"Sure." Carefully I put one foot in front of the other. As I reached the green court I wondered what on earth I was going to do. "I don't have a racket."

"Here. I'll show you how to use my racket and then toss balls for you to hit." He handed me his racket and then motioned for me to come closer.

"Where?" I asked as I moved toward him.

"Here."

"But you're standing there."

"Okay, okay. Just turn around and stand where you are."

I was getting the creeps. I didn't even want my father to teach me tennis this close. "Why don't you just toss me balls? I learn fast."

"Okay. Just stand like this with your side to the net and swing. See. Like this. Follow through."

I tried a few practice shots. "Like this?"

"Yeah." Scotty came over and touched my racket, then my elbow. "Okay. You've got the idea."

I guess I lost the idea, because after a while Scotty Dumont was yelling at me. "No, Meredith, keep your wrist straight!"

"You can stop right now, Scotty Dumont!" I loved his name, but I said it firmly. At that moment I was very fed up. "I don't need you getting angry at me."

"I'm not angry."

"It sounds like it to me. And you're impatient."

"That's because . . ." He looked over at his brother. The backboard was going thud, thud.

"Because I don't learn so fast?" I guessed.

"I didn't say that. You're just extrasensitive."

"I'm just somebody you can boss around."

"Baloney."

"I don't care if I never get on any tennis team in the entire world."

"Neither do I!" He threw a tennis ball and it whizzed right by me. Then another. He looked like an ace pitcher. "Girls," he muttered.

I could have whacked him over the head with his own racket. I don't know why. He sort of reminded me of Dad when he yelled at me. I set his racket down on the grass. I didn't want to say a word, but I wanted him to say something. I don't know what. I walked slowly out the gate, to the street, determined in all that loud silence to look proud.

"B'Bye, Baby Cat!" he suddenly shouted.

Now that really did hurt. But I didn't turn around. I started to run. My whole day had become one big mess.

I got my notebook when I got home and sat on the patio. I was in the middle of a letter to Grandma when a truck, shiny red, rolled by and then backed up from the stop sign. Scotty jumped out. I thought about running inside, but I didn't. Being called "Baby Cat" had hurt too much to act like a baby.

"Hi, Scotty," I said. I was embarrassed, but somehow I found strength to speak.

"Hi, Meredith. I'm sorry for calling you a baby."

"Thanks. I guess maybe I *am* too sensitive."

"Maybe." He paused. "Well, I guess I'll see you in school."

"Right."

He dashed back to the truck. I daydreamed for a couple minutes after he left and then picked up my notebook to finish my letter.

November 1

Dear Grandma,

I don't know what got into me just now. Scotty was trying to teach me tennis and I ended up being my disagreeable self again. I feel I surely must have a very uncharitable, disagreeable

58

sort of heart. Nothing like a fountain at all. What do you think?

Do Buddhists always have to be good? Please find out if God takes Buddhists at twelve or am I too young to train.

Do you ever think I'll be good and kind all the way through? I can feel so irritable without knowing why and end up getting into trouble. Please pray for me.

Love, Meredith

Mom and Dad and Adam stopped and got hamburgers for dinner. That almost always makes my day. I was glad to see them, Dad in particular.

"Dad . . ." I said through a mouthful of french fries.

"Yeah?"

I took a swig of milk to clean my mouth and braces. "Will you *really* teach me tennis?"

"Sure."

"Without getting angry?"

There was a pause. "I can try."

"Good." I looked at him with serious eyes. "And when no one else is at the park?"

"Without getting angry and when no one else is at the park. Cross my heart."

"So," I said, glad to have that settled. "How was Tina?"

"Good," Mom said. "She's got a boyfriend." I saw a look go between Mom and Dad that I didn't quite understand.

"Great! What's he like?"

"He's real nice looking," my mother answered.

"Too old," Dad said.

"A senior," Mom explained.

"A senior," I shrieked. I was happy for Tina. Her decision to go to a deaf school was giving her her first boyfriend. "We have to get a teletypewriter now for sure."

"Maybe," Dad said.

"You said . . ."

"Meredith," Mom interrupted. "I found out that the Theatre of the Deaf will be here the Friday after Thanksgiving. Tina wants to go. I thought we'd all go and maybe you could bring Charlotte Ann."

"Sure," I said, really not feeling too sure what I felt about that, remembering how Charlotte Ann had laughed at the idea of Tina becoming an actress. "I'll ask her tomorrow at school."

Chapter · 8 ·

"Well, I don't know" was Charlotte Ann's response when I invited her to go see the Theatre of the Deaf perform. We were walking to gym class.

"*Por qué?*" I asked, practicing my Spanish.

"*Porque* it might just be too weird for me."

"How can it be any more weird than your own family?"

Charlotte Ann punched me, harder than I thought necessary, harder than a just-for-fun punch. "Ouch! I'll be black and blue!"

"Ooo, poor Meredith. Maybe Scotty will kiss your arm then."

I was thinking about hitting her with the books I was carrying when her brother, Pete, walked by.

"Hi, Mama Cat." He took off, but not before I managed to get him in his lower back with the edge of my notebook.

"See what I mean, Charlotte Ann?" I pointed out. "You live with a fourteen-year-old who acts like he's ten, or seven. How weird can you get?"

"He's fifteen."

"What?"

"Yeah. He failed fifth grade."

"You're kidding."

"No. But, Meredith, I wouldn't tease him about it. He'll kill you or make your life miserable, and I'm not sure which is worse."

"I get the idea." I paused and started in again. "The play's really not that weird, Charlotte Ann. I know."

"Have you gone before?"

"No. But my folks and Tina went in Chicago."

"How come you didn't go?"

"It was a long time ago. I got to stay with my grandma. That's when Tina got the idea of becoming an actress."

"Too weird."

"Come on, Charlotte Ann. We could get all dressed up. You like to do that once in a while, don't you? Maybe we could get a hot fudge sundae afterward."

"Too weird."

I let her be. Actually, I guess I really sort of gave her the cold shoulder. I changed that cold-shoulder attitude, though, when I got some time on the bench in the basketball game during gym. Charlotte Ann was playing. Near me, Claire Ellen, who was wearing her cheerleader outfit, even though it made Coach Matthews angry, nodded in Charlotte Ann's direction and said, "Now there's a child no mother could love."

"What d'you mean?" a girl named Sarah Jane asked. I didn't understand either, but I wasn't part of the conversation. I wasn't part of that glamor crowd of cheerleaders and student council representatives. And I knew that had nothing to do with my being new at Crockett.

"I mean she's *so* ugly."

I still wanted to know what Claire Ellen meant. I didn't think Charlotte Ann was ugly. She was scrawny, but I knew she was really a strong, determined person. And for some reason that I didn't understand, she had deep worry lines on her forehead and between her eyebrows, as if she was always having to think, and think hard, but I wouldn't say that made her ugly, just a little cross-looking. With people saying those kinds of things about her,

Charlotte Ann certainly didn't need a cold shoulder from a friend.

In Spanish class Charlotte Ann leaned across the desk and whispered, *"Vengo a teatro."*

"Por qué? Helado?" I figured she couldn't resist the promise of ice cream.

"Sí, y curioso." She was coming because she wanted the ice cream and because she was curious. Me too. We weren't that different. I wondered what Claire Ellen would have to say about how *I* looked.

Mom and Adam brought Tina home the Wednesday before Thanksgiving. I was glad to have her home. I was so glad, I cleaned every inch of our room. I especially wanted to show her how I was doing with tennis, and to find out about her boyfriend.

"Room looks good," Tina signed as she looked around our room.

"Thanks."

"Come see my room." Adam tugged at Tina's hand.

"Can I unpack your things?" I asked Tina as she was dragged from the room.

"Sure."

I had cleaned out a couple drawers that were supposed to be Tina's anyway. At first I was going to leave half the drawers for her in case she came back, but my things thoughtlessly kept multiplying and spilling over into empty drawers.

Between two of her sweaters I found a photograph of a boy. I stared at him up close and then at arm's length. He had brown wavy hair and a sort of square face. He was rugged, almost manly. Cute would not be accurate. Tina's boyfriend looked much more grown-up than I expected. I stood the photo on the dresser so that it faced her side of the bed. When she came back I asked her about her boyfriend.

"Russell," she said.

"Russell? You call him Russ?"

"No. Not Rusty either. Russell. He's very tall." She put her hand about a foot above her head.

"Six feet two inches," I guessed.

She put her arms across her chest, which I think is a lot more understandable than the word "love," and then added her own sign, a swaying, waltzing motion. She was in love. "Maybe marry someday," she signed.

I was startled. I figured she'd have trouble with Dad if it was going to be any time soon. Maybe Mom too. "Going to college first?" I asked.

"I don't know now."

Mom and Dad wanted Tina to go to Gallaudet, the college for the deaf in Washington, D.C. We had all the makings for a big blowup here, so I decided not to give away her secret.

Thanksgiving was a warm day. Dad hooked up the turkey on a motorized spit over charcoal and basted it with some lemon and orange syrup. I also got a long tennis lesson early in the morning when the courts were empty. Tina came along.

"You're doing really well, Meredith," Dad said as he swung an easy shot at me. "We'll have to get you your own racket."

I was using Mom's racket from college. "I'd like that."

"Maybe for Christmas."

I was finally beginning to catch on to shifting my position on the court quickly enough. My father had yelled "move your feet" probably a thousand times before the words really sunk in. I didn't hold that yelling against him, because it did get me moving. I didn't like it, but I could see that he really didn't mean anything hurtful by it.

Every once in a while during our practice I glanced at Tina. She sat on the bench and gazed around, looking full of bliss. I guessed I was seeing a case of first love.

I thought nothing much was going to happen the day after Thanksgiving except that we'd all sit around feeling bloated, eat leftovers, and then go to the play. But something did happen. It was my mother's idea that we get a kitten, snow white with splotches of rust and dark brown. Now Adam and I had a real cat to take to the park. We called her "Angel" because my father, who wasn't exactly keen on the idea of a cat in the house, had said she'd better not make any trouble.

Charlotte Ann called me a little later in the afternoon with a question. "Are you going to get dressed up for the play?"

"Sure. I have this holiday sort of dress. I wear it around Christmastime."

"What's it like?"

"A deep green velvet jumper. I wear it with a white silky blouse. Why?"

"It sounds nice."

"Thanks. You can wear whatever you want."

"I don't have much that's dressy. Grandma learned I was going out, and she made me these black pants."

"Sounds nice."

"They're silk."

"Oh, Charlotte Ann. That's wonderful."

"And Meredith."

"Yeah?"

"She got me this soft, fluffy white turtleneck."

"That sounds perfect."

"Do you think so?"

"Sure."

"I was really surprised."

I wasn't surprised. "That's how grandmas are," I said.

We had a big shock when we got to the theater. We all met Russell. Boy, was he handsome. And big. He drove in from his folk's ranch about forty miles south of San Antonio. He kissed Tina right away, right in front of us all.

For a second I let my imagination run wild. I imagined Tina in a wedding gown, Russell in a tuxedo. It all seemed real normal. I could see Tina with a baby in her arms. Even wondering whether their babies would be deaf didn't bother me. I could see they would be able to take care of whatever happened. And I'd make a fantastic aunt. I just knew it.

We all shook hands with Russell and talked briefly about the school, the holidays, what year he was in school, even though we all knew. When Russell and Tina went to visit with some of their deaf friends from school, Mom and Dad started whispering.

"What'd you think, Charlotte Ann?" I asked as soon as Tina and Russell had left us.

She looked around. "It's a little scary."

"Maybe at first." I looked around the theater lobby too. "And we're in the minority." People were signing everywhere, excited and friendly, the way I had come to know the deaf. "They're real friendly."

"Uh-huh" was all Charlotte Ann said.

The theater group did a play about King Arthur's court—the knights and their search for the Holy Grail. There was this one fantastic talking horse. There was a lot of laughing in the audience, the loud laughing I had heard from the deaf before. It was very comforting somehow. Every once in a while in the play one of the actors would talk about his own life, stepping out of character. That was more serious, but it was still a good evening of entertainment, and we all learned a lot.

November 25

Dear Grandma,
Meeting Russell was a great surprise. I should have guessed he'd be there, but Tina's always liked to surprise hearing people, even her own family.

I liked the play a lot—and I know Tina can do just as well someday. And I think Charlotte Ann knows that, too, now. She learned a lot about the deaf and I learned a lot about her.

I learned Charlotte Ann isn't as tough as she tries to let on. She's sort of a softie like me. She cried because the play was so beautiful. When she cried so hard her glasses wouldn't stay on, it was hard to know what to do. Finally she told me she was crying about her younger sister, who's retarded and living at the state school in Austin. She said she'd never talked about her with anyone because nobody ever understood how she felt. It tore her up, she said, to care so much yet be able to do so little to help. I understood that.

This was a secret, though, she really needed to share. She looked so peaceful afterward. I felt happy for you and for Charlotte Ann and for me. It was a happiness that bubbled like a fountain, Grandma, and I felt blessed to have had such good company as you and Charlotte Ann. Now it can't be selfish to feel blessed, can it?

Love ya,
Meredith

Chapter • 9 •

After Thanksgiving I practiced tennis every day, either with Dad or against the backboard. Sometimes I'd take a pail of balls up to the courts after school to practice my serve. I wasn't quite sure what my goal was—to get on the tennis team, to make Scotty notice me in a sparkly sort of way, or to show Peter a thing or two. It didn't seem to matter. I was becoming an athletic, outdoors sort of person.

I was glad it didn't snow in San Antonio, because the weather made my practice sessions possible. Still, balmy breezes in early December did not seem Christmassy. "What are we going to do about Christmas?" I asked one evening.

"We're not going to have it," Dad said from behind his newspaper.

"You're kidding."

"He's kidding, Meredith," Mom reassured me. "We'll have Christmas as usual."

"But there's no snow."

"It'll probably be the best Christmas you've ever had," Dad said. "We'll have a regular tennis clinic around here."

"I remember reading about Christmas in San Antonio in the

travel section of the *Sun-Times* last year," Mom said. "It's actually one of the most interesting places in the country at Christmastime. The article described how the banks of the San Antonio river are decorated with colorful Christmas lights while barges full of people singing Christmas carols float on the river." Mother also remembered something about a mariachi Mass and a pageant at a mission church. "And I think on Christmas Eve people break piñatas and make tamales."

This was the part that interested me, the part about the piñatas. "Where do you buy piñatas?" I asked.

"In Mexico," Dad answered.

"Do we have to go that far?"

"Well, actually, I think I've seen them at the market downtown," he said, "and in some of the shops along the river."

Suddenly Mom stood up. Something was on her mind. "Don't go away, Mom," I said. I was enjoying talking with my parents.

"I'll be right back. I want to see if I can find a tamale recipe." I looked at Dad. We both knew we wouldn't hear from her for a while.

"Do you think she's ever going back to work?" I whispered.

He laughed. "Does your stomach need a rest?"

"No. I like things spicy."

"Well, she's looking for a job. She's gotten one job offer already, but she hasn't made a decision."

I didn't like the sound of that, or how things in my house kept happening without anyone asking me what I thought. "Hey, Mom!" I shouted.

"Yeah?" she answered from the kitchen.

"Don't go back to work."

"Well, I can't for a while. I have to take the bar exam in February and then wait for the results. I did get a job offer to start work right after that, but I told the firm I wanted to wait till June. They're supposed to get back to me."

I felt that panicky sensation I get when I want things to be different yet know that because I'm twelve I have little influence. I liked my mother not working. It made our house feel more like a home, someplace I wanted to come to when school was over for the day. Summer vacations and holidays seemed a better deal to me if Mom was home. Things were a lot less hurried. "I mean *never*. I want you never to go back to work."

"Ssh," Dad said softly. "Adam's asleep."

I went quickly to the kitchen. "I need you here."

"Well, you've got me here for the next six months anyway. I like being here at home. But I like working away from home, too, honey. I've always gotten a lot of satisfaction from work."

"Don't go." Tears came to my eyes.

Mom reached out and hugged me right away. "I enjoy your company too, honey. But I don't understand, Meredith. You're in school most of the day. And you did fine all those years . . ." Her voice trailed off and she hugged me harder.

I shook my head as if to say again, "Don't go back to work." I also meant that I was surprised at my feelings. I'd always accepted her working full-time. Lots of mothers work. That's just the way things are. I guess knowing what it was like to have her home made me want her there.

"I've been thinking of opening an office near here." Mom said. "I wouldn't go in all the time. Would you like that?"

"That sounds better."

"I sort of like the idea too. But something's wrong, Meredith. You've always been so independent."

"It's just . . . I wish things were normal. A normal mother. A normal sister. Just normal." I couldn't hold back my tears, but I wasn't crying about normality. It seemed as if I was angry and sad and lonely, all at once.

"Oh, Meredith, honey."

I was glad she didn't ask me some question like "What's nor-

mal?" or blame me for being an empty-headed, trouble-making
teenager, which is what a lot of parents think about adolescents.
Or worse yet, say that everything and everyone was normal but
me. She just held me in a way that almost made me feel she could
absorb my troubled feelings.

The phone rang and Dad answered. "It's for you, Meredith.
It's Charlotte Ann. Can you talk?"

"Sure," I said, wiping my nose with the back of my hand. I
took the receiver. "Hi, Charlotte Ann."

"Are you okay, Meredith? You sound kind of funny."

"Of course I'm okay." Of course I wasn't, but I didn't want
to explain.

"Did you get your homework done?"

"Yeah. I had to turn the TV off to do it though."

"Me too. All that reading for Texas History was boring."

"Pretty too boring." That was Adam's expression, "pretty
too." I liked how it combined what adults said to him.

"Meredith, Grandma wants to know if you can go downtown
to the river this Saturday. She'd take us by bus on her way to
work."

"Why?"

"To shop for Christmas. Then to walk along the river."

"Where does she work? I didn't know she had a job."

"Just a job."

"That's neat. Downtown and all."

"She cleans offices if you really want to know. That's all,
Meredith. Nothing neat."

"I think that's neat." I could almost feel Charlotte Ann roll her
eyes. "Neat" was another word like "normal"—everybody's ideas
were different.

"Let me ask my mom." Mom thought the idea was great. I'd
be the first in the family to see downtown decorated for Christmas.

"Charlotte Ann?"

"Yeah."

"I can go. How late will we stay?"

"Grandma wants to take us to dinner.

"But on what she earns . . ."

"She really wants to, Meredith. Can you be here at nine? The bus comes around nine-fifteen."

"Sure."

"I'm glad you're coming. Grandma will be real happy. I gotta go now."

"Thanks, Charlotte Ann."

"Sure."

Charlotte Ann and her grandmother were standing under a palm tree at the bus stop when I arrived Saturday morning. Her grandmother was dressed in baggy lime green pants, less than full-length. I guess you could call them knickers, but not quite. Her shoulder-length silver hair was loosely braided into two pigtails, held in place by wide lime green ribbons that dangled down her back. What caught my eyes even more than all the lime green was the hot pink rain slicker she wore, cut at the waist and trimmed with black at the cuffs, the bottom, and the place where the zipper should have been. Under the rain gear she wore a flannel shirt, mostly red, not tucked into her pants but tied at her waist, which was slightly plump. I thought I caught sight of underwear, like a man's T-shirt, beneath the flannel shirt. Her arms held a grocery sack as if it were a baby.

"She's got a change of clothes in that sack," Charlotte Ann explained in a whisper when we boarded the bus. "I'm sorry she looks like she does."

"I don't mind."

"Yes you do."

"No, really."

"Yes you do." Charlotte Ann's voice was insistent and I gave up.

The bus was filled with holiday shoppers. Grandma sat down in the last vacant seat for two and moved as far toward the window as she could, as if she thought we all three might fit. Charlotte Ann headed for the back of the bus. I shushed at her but she kept trudging along. It seemed hard to decide whether to follow my best friend or sit next to Grandma. Torn, I swung into the seat next to Grandma. I figured she wouldn't have moved to the window if she hadn't hoped for us to sit by her.

My heart aches when people hope for something like that from me. It seems so cruel to want to ignore a wish when I can see it right in front of my eyes. My grandmother said it was feeling the loving light when you granted a wish. To do otherwise would be mean.

Charlotte Ann came back toward us, but didn't sit with us. I could tell she was nearby, because I heard her muttering. I figured her forehead was all wrinkled again, but I didn't turn around.

Someone at the back of the bus had a radio tuned to a station playing Christmas carols. It was nice background music. Then Charlotte Ann's grandma began to sing along.

Right away Charlotte Ann came and stood next to us. Now it was her turn to do the shushing, but her grandmother wouldn't stop. I looked up at Charlotte Ann. She rolled her eyes up toward the ceiling, bit her lip, and sucked in a deep breath. "Grandma, please," she whispered with great determination, the kind of determination that people have who think they can clean up the world's problems with a broom. "This isn't home."

Grandma looked at her. "You're at home wherever you feel safe." Then she sang even louder, and now two men up front joined in. Three boys standing by the back door snickered. I could feel Charlotte Ann cringe.

"*We're* safe as long as 'O Holy Night' doesn't come on," Charlotte Ann whispered in my ear.

But sure enough, it did come on, two carols later. By then almost half the bus, including me, was singing. But Grandma carried the day. She had a great voice, and I told her so when the song ended.

"I love opera," she explained. "I sing along with the radio all the time." She looked at Charlotte Ann. "And I come from a family where you have to shout to get any attention."

"Geez, Grandma" was Charlotte Ann's response. But somehow she looked as proud of her grandmother as embarrassed.

The bus came to a stop and everyone stood. We were at the end of the line, downtown, in front of the Alamo.

Grandma walked with us around the enormous decorated Christmas tree in the plaza. "We'll see this lit up if we stay long enough tonight," she said.

"Sure. I'd like that. My mom read about this tree in a Chicago newspaper," I said.

Grandma looked at her watch. "I have to go. I'll meet you here at four."

Charlotte Ann nodded, and I automatically flicked my forehead with my forefinger. As Grandma moved quickly away Charlotte Ann nudged me. "What was that?" she asked.

"A sign."

"For what?"

"A sign that I understand."

"You talk with your hands?"

"My whole family does. We have to. Don't you remember from the theater?" I giggled then as I started to do a Hawaiian hula imitation, using my hands as flamboyantly as possible. I wanted to see if Charlotte Ann only got upset at her grandmother, or if friends could embarrass her as easily.

"Oh, Meredith." Charlotte Ann swung her purse at me. "Not in public. Be serious."

"I am." I kept dancing, slowly circling the Christmas tree, doing what I figured was a ballet step. And then, before my very eyes, Charlotte Ann began to hula, too. I was glad to see her silly side come out and shine. We did all sorts of motions with hands and arms as we moved sideways round the tree. Tourists and shoppers walked by without giving us any particular notice. I guess they were too preoccupied with shopping to wonder at our craziness.

Charlotte Ann started a giggle that was contagious. Suddenly she stopped. "Oh, oh."

That stopped me too. "What?"

"I have to pee. Don't laugh anymore."

There was a hotel across the street, and we made a mad dash for the lobby. A fountain came into view as we scurried down the steps. "Oh-oh. Water," Charlotte Ann said, and we dangerously giggled some more. She stopped at one point and we both acted very serious. Then we scurried again, having no time to appreciate the mosaics or water or landscaping. I could sense that it was beautiful, though, with the sky a perfect robin's egg blue and the air warm and crystal clear. We were going to have a great day.

After a successful bathroom stop we recrossed the street. "I want to go to the candy counter at Joske's before anything else," Charlotte Ann said. I followed her, completely captivated by the prospect of fun. We each got chocolate—Charlotte Ann got some turtles and I got fudge. Then we combed every area of Joske's, a large department store next to the Alamo. I saw some gift possibilities, but bought nothing. Mostly we tried on things for ourselves.

"Buy it," I said when Charlotte Ann tried on a headband with feathers that dangled at her temples.

"You're kidding."

"No. How much is it?"

"Twenty-six dollars."

"I'm kidding."

Then we explored every inch of the river—shops full of pottery, turquoise, and silver jewelry, wall hangings from Pakistan, tourist junk. I got a cowboy hat for Adam. I wanted to get a piñata for Dad, and when Charlotte Ann offered to take turns carrying it, I bought one—a colorful purple and red parrot.

At two we spotted an ice cream shop and decided to rest our feet. We both wanted chocolate almond, but I decided to get the praline cream just for variety.

"I have an idea, Meredith," Charlotte Ann began.

"Oh, yeah?"

"Yeah. For a club."

I didn't say anything.

"Aren't you interested?" Charlotte Ann asked.

"Clubs make me nervous."

"Why?"

"They're too much work, I guess." I didn't tell her they made me nervous because they tried to make everyone think or feel the same way. I had too much disagreement in me to be a good club member.

"Well, I was thinking about a club for kids like us who have a handicapped brother or sister."

The idea was so weird I wondered why I hadn't thought of it myself. "Hmmm" was all I could say.

"What do you think?"

"But why?"

"To talk. You know. Talk about what it's like, what you feel, how your parents get. It would be like one of those support groups adults are always setting up for themselves. It would be an adult thing to do."

"Uh-huh."

"Why things like that happen." The excitement in Charlotte Ann's voice trickled off slightly. She seemed to swallow hard then, and I understood why. Tina coped very well, and there were medical reasons why she was deaf, but the ultimate why of her handicap, or why any other kind of suffering happened, was hard to understand or accept.

"Sure." I sat forward. I felt a lot of kindness for Charlotte Ann at that moment, even if I didn't like clubs much. "Do you want a lick?" I reached my cone across and then I got a taste of hers, chocolate with a big piece of almond. "I think it's a good idea. But how do you advertise for something like that?"

"Well, I know Janie Rodriquez has a mentally retarded older brother and Sammy Taylor has a sister with cerebral palsy. Will you help, Meredith?"

"I guess." I knew the club would help Charlotte Ann, and I'd do just about anything for her. "It would be nice to get to know some other kids better. You're my best friend, Charlotte Ann, but it wouldn't be bad for me to have, well . . ." I didn't want Charlotte Ann to get the idea that I thought she wasn't friend enough for me.

"You don't have to explain. I know what you mean, Meredith."

"And if it doesn't work out, if the other kids aren't interested, let's just you and me talk," I suggested. Then I thought for a minute. "I don't think we should start the club till after Christmas vacation, though. It's sort of serious business and Christmas is for fun." I had doubts about this kind of club. But I didn't want to take away Charlotte Ann's interest now that her secret about having a retarded sister was out in the open.

"Sure. It can wait."

We finished our cones and then Charlotte Ann talked till almost four. I found out that her father had wanted to keep her little sister, Joanna, hidden in the trailer and that's why her parents got a divorce. Her grandmother came to live with them to care for Joanna at home, but now her sister was at the state school.

At four, Grandma was waiting at the tree in front of the Alamo. She had changed into a lime green dress with a dark green wool jacket decorated with a wreath pin. I gave her a Joske's shopping bag with a brightly colored reindeer leaping through a midnight blue starry sky, for her other clothes.

"You look lovely," I said.

"Thanks."

"Tell me the sign for love," Charlotte Ann said.

I put my arms across my chest. "Love," I said. And then I signed an "L" and then a "Y". "Love-ly."

"That's nice." Charlotte Ann looked at me. "It's like it's more real than the word."

"Sometimes it seems that way."

We ended up going to a place on the river that served both Mexican and Italian food. And then for a couple of hours we walked along the river. Christmas lights were everywhere, in trees and windows, along the walkway and bridges, around cafés, boutiques, clubs. Dance music filled the air and mingled with Christmas carols. For a while we followed some strolling carolers. At one point another group of carolers floated by on a barge and the two groups sang "Silent Night" together.

Charlotte Ann and I each held one of Grandma's arms as we climbed the steps of the hotel where we had thankfully found the bathroom at the beginning of our day. We were giggling and huffing and puffing, shopping bags and the parrot piñata swinging at our sides.

Suddenly the Alamo's enormous Christmas tree appeared, full of glorious colored lights. We stood still for a minute, completely captured by its shimmering beauty. "It's beautiful," Grandma said.

"That must be what we all look like when we get to heaven. Can you imagine that?"

I could. I liked that idea a lot. I was going to tell them about my star theory, that we each become a star when we die, but I wasn't really in the mood to talk about death.

We charged across the street. Grandma began singing "Jingle Bells," and Charlotte Ann and I joined in at the top of our lungs. We had only a couple of minutes to promenade around the tree before the bus came. We sang all the way home, one carol after another, but this time the bus had few passengers and we sang alone.

Mom was waiting for me when we got back to the motel, the beam from its lighthouse sending out a safe, homey glow.

"Thanks," I said to Grandma. "I had a great time." I reached out my hand. Grandma smiled at me and reached out for a hug. I hugged back. She was squishy, too, and the hug felt real good.

"See ya, Charlotte Ann."

"See ya, Meredith."

As we pulled out, I saw them walk off, arm in arm, swaying to "Joy to the World." It would sure hurt not having my grandma around for Christmas, but seeing Charlotte Ann get closer to hers made me feel very good.

Chapter · 10 ·

December 25

Dear Grandma,

Today is Christmas. I'm sure you celebrate even more than us. Or do you? Have you seen Jesus and do you have a pageant? I'm sure in heaven it would be quite spectacular.

Adam played "The Star" in the nativity pageant last night. He was a real ham, holding the star high above his head and swaying back and forth as he came down the aisle. Remember the year when I was Mary and you wore that nice red silk dress?

I've been working on the fountain idea quite a bit lately. I drew a bunch in my sketchbook, different sizes and shapes. In my imagination they all sparkle with rainbow colors. They keep flowing and they keep sparkling. I'm not sure where the beginning of the flow is. Is the beginning there in heaven?

I miss you, Grandma. I got a lump in my throat opening gifts and remembering you sitting with the afghan around your shoulders last year. I really didn't think you'd die. I'd never known anybody who was so special who died. I think last Christmas I believed you loved us so much and we loved you so much that you'd recover.

It's real mild here today. Must be seventy-five degrees.

81

Dad just called for a tennis game so I can try out my great new
tennis racket. Merry Christmas!

Love, Meredith

Christmas vacation ended too quickly. Dad took some time off
and we had a regular tennis clinic going for almost two weeks. My
tennis game really improved. And I think all my tennis playing
helped keep me from gaining weight.

Pete came up to me that first day back at school and I was glad
to see him. Charlotte Ann was not in school and I wondered what
had happened. It was strange not to have her by my side in the
hall between classes.

"She got real sick last night," he explained. "I guess she didn't
want to come back to school. I wouldn't if I were her, either. I
hear you two are going to start a club for crips."

"What?"

"A club for crips. You know. Crippled people. You want to
hear about this new Helen Keller doll that's on the market?
It . . ."

I walked quickly away, straight as a board, as if getting stiff
like that would save me from Pete's abuse.

"Hey, everyone," Pete yelled. The hall was crowded and he
got a lot of attention. "Got any crippled retards for Meredith's
club?"

My spine burned and I felt red heat quickly inch to my neck,
my jaw, and then my eyes. It didn't help that Scotty was within
easy earshot of Pete's comments.

"There goes Miss Puritan, Miss Goody Two-Shoes," Pete
called out as I quickened my pace. And then he shouted, "Crip
lover."

I raced to the cafeteria. I wasn't hungry anymore, but sitting
still and acting as if I was about to eat somehow made me feel safe
from Pete.

"Meredith."

I turned from my lunch. It was Scotty.

"Can I sit here? I mean, I know Charlotte Ann's not here."

"Sure." I watched him mount the chair like a horse. He was wearing jeans and cowboy boots. I felt a strange sensation, like a feather fluttering in my stomach, as he turned his carton of milk back and forth. I moved my elbow closer to my own body. I was a little afraid I was going to let myself touch or bump him and I didn't want him to get any ideas. I also didn't want to remind him of how awkward I'd been on the tennis court that day he'd tried to teach me to play.

"Are you and Charlotte Ann starting a club?" he asked.

"Maybe. It's none of Pete's business what we're doing. Why do you want to know?"

"Well, I've never heard of anyone just starting a club here all from scratch. It took Pete over a year to get approval for the tennis club, but maybe that was just Pete. He's sort of slow, you know."

I nodded. I had a whole bunch of other words to describe Pete, but I held my tongue.

"Your club does seem sort of different from anything else around here."

"Weird?"

He shrugged. "I guess you could say that."

"It's contagious. You'd better not sit here."

Scotty laughed. "Maybe it'd do me good to get weird. How do I know?"

"Pete will give you a hard time."

"He gives everybody a hard time. He thinks that's being macho or something. It's part of his athletic image. So what's this club all about?"

"Oh, it's just an idea. It would be for kids who have brothers or sisters who are handicapped. Then they could talk things over.

Otherwise, it's pretty much something nobody wants to discuss."

"Benjie Clark's younger brother is blind. Maybe he'd like something like your club."

"Who's he?"

"He's in eighth grade. I'll introduce you."

"Thanks, Scotty."

"Sure. I probably know a couple others. I know LuAnn Simpson's older sister went schizophrenic and was in the state hospital for a while and now she's at home. It's been real hard for LuAnn. Do you want some help getting other members?"

"You want to get *that* weird?"

"Sure. I'll see what I'm missing. Maybe I'll really like being *that* weird."

"Okay." I was surprised, and very touched. It was a generosity I didn't expect in a boy, especially a cute boy.

"I'll make a list tonight. We can meet at lunch tomorrow, with Charlotte Ann if she's back."

Charlotte Ann didn't come to school for two more days. I talked with her on the phone and she gave me four names. And Scotty introduced me to four of his friends. Besides Benjie Clark, Amanda Cruz had a sister who was blind. I met LuAnn Simpson and then Janie Rodriquez and Sammy Taylor, whom Charlotte Ann had told me about before Christmas. I liked them right away. Janie had a younger sister who was just learning sign language. Barbara Jane Evans had a sister who was paralyzed because of a fall from a horse. Sue Ellen Matthews' little brother had leukemia, and though I thought that was different, she wanted to join so badly that I let her. Finally, there was Bobby Jo Henderson. His older brother had been in a motorcycle accident and was a paraplegic.

When Charlotte Ann got to school on Thursday, we went straight to the library to see if we could hold our first meeting there. The librarian, Ms. Lawson, was very excited about what she called our "support group" and said we could have the library after school the next Friday, a little more than a week away.

Everything went fine through the first fifteen minutes of our meeting that next week. I was surprised that all ten of us showed up. Ms. Lawson said she might be able to bring in speakers, counselors, and doctors, to give us information and answer questions. We were trying to think up a name for our club when Mr. Howard interrupted. He's a school counselor who's also in charge of clubs and things like student council elections.

"I've heard by way of the grapevine that we have a new club here," he said. He smiled big.

"Yes," I said. "We don't have a name yet."

"Well, I'm here to inform you that you just can't form a club like this. It has to be approved by a committee if it's going to be an official club, and given a sponsor."

"I'll be glad to be the sponsor . . ." Ms. Lawson began.

"And your club isn't a proper school club from what Peter Kincaid tells me. It's not related to school functions or school goals. We have handicapped access here so there's really no need. The club is just personal and not related to the school in any way. There's no need for it, so you children will have to leave."

"Children . . ." Ms. Lawson's eyes grew wide. I could tell she was angry. I was angry myself. Hurt too. I felt embarrassed.

"There's no rule preventing us," Janie said.

"Yes," Mr. Howard said, "there is a rule if you're going to meet on school premises and be an official school club. If anything happened, the school would be held accountable. We need to know what's going on. That's why you need approval."

"I'm sure we can get approval," I said.

"You can try to get approval. But for now you must vacate the library."

"How about if we call ourselves a support group?" I asked.

"Sorry, but I haven't time to argue this any longer." He stood still, full of impatience and something close to fury. We got up slowly and filed out.

"It doesn't seem right." Benjie kicked a rock across the yard.

With his Texas drawl, Bobby Jo cursed a blue streak, all aimed at Mr. Howard. None of us minded his language. To my mind a Southern accent added such a lovely lilt that everything was melodic in one way or another, even cursing. Completely disgruntled, almost in shock, we sat down on cement benches near the parking lot to wait for rides.

"We could meet privately," Amanda suggested. "You know, in homes."

"That's too much of a hassle," Benjie said. "I'd have all sorts of transportation problems."

"Me too," Sammy agreed.

"We don't have to be a club after all," Charlotte Ann said slowly, as if her idea was coming to her one word at a time. "We could sit together at lunch and not call ourselves anything. We'd just be friends. There can't be a rule against that." Her eyes were wide and bright as she looked around at us.

"Yeah, friends," I agreed. "There's ten of us. That's the size of a table. Does everyone have early lunch?"

"Not me." It was Benjie. "But I think I can change gym. Let me talk to Coach Alvarez."

"I think this may all work out." Charlotte Ann sighed with relief and I patted her back. I knew she wanted this support group probably more than anyone had ever wanted a silly old club at our school.

"It'll work out, Charlotte Ann. Don't worry. Getting together's a good idea." I was happy for her because actually she seemed less worried than ever. I thought I saw a fountain in her flow out

to all of us, a fountain that came from a heart that really cared
and eyes that sparkled more brightly than usual.

I always knew my grandmother understood a lot. Right then,
watching Charlotte Ann, I decided that every one of us has a
fountain, which makes us all alike. Some people keep theirs bot-
tled up, others share. Charlotte Ann's was uncorked now that her
secret about her sister was in the open.

January 22

Dear Grandma,

Today was a big disappointment as far as adults go. Not
all adults. Just adults who make a lot of rules and take them seriously so they can feel big and important, like they know what's
best.

All because of someone like that—Mr. Howard, to be
precise—we couldn't form a club to talk about our brothers and
sisters who are handicapped, to understand them and ourselves
better.

I guess he didn't exactly say we couldn't form a club. We
just can't meet like one at the school. So we're going to meet at
lunch. Now that idea I like. I like to talk just about as much as
I like to eat!

I think I'm seeing more about fountains. Charlotte Ann's
been a help. I think my fountain is my heart and when there's love
bubbling in my heart and flowing out to others then my heart and
me are blessed. Am I right?

Take care of yourself.

Love from Mama Cat

Benjie got help from both Ms. Lawson and Charlotte Ann's
mom, and his schedule was changed, so by Tuesday all ten of us
were at the same table. Mostly we were investigating each other's

lunches, giggling and getting to know one another just like any other table in the large, noisy cafeteria. I wasn't sure we'd do anything more than that.

"You know," Janie Rodriquez said, "the best part is knowing you're not alone, that there are other families who have the same kinds of problems."

"I know," said Bobby Jo. "My father doesn't let us talk about my brother at all. I think he feels guilty, but it would help him if he talked."

Suddenly everything was interrupted.

"So. Here's the little crip society of America, huh?" It was Pete, moving around our table like a hulking quarterback. "Give me a little 'let's-hear-one-for-the-rejects' cheer, huh, guys?"

I looked at Charlotte Ann. She was turning red. It looked like an angry red rather than an embarrassed red. "Sit down, Peter," Charlotte Ann ordered. "Maybe you'll learn something."

"Sit down, Peter," he mimicked. "You guys are so weird you're going to end up as rejects too. Reject table!" he shouted. "Come see a bunch of rejects."

A hush fell over our side of the cafeteria. I could hear people mumbling. In the distance it seemed that the usual hubbub continued. I saw Ms. Lawson get up from the teachers' table. Then I saw Scotty.

"Hey, Pete." Scotty took hold of Pete's arm. Pete forcefully shook him off. I stopped breathing. It looked as if there was going to be a fight.

"Got any crippled horses, Scotty, for these weirdos to moan and groan over?"

"A crippled horse gets put out of its misery. Maybe they're just trying to find some peace for theirs. Ever think about anybody else but yourself, Pete?" No one at our table moved.

"Yeah. I think about normal people, normal things. Teammates. They're normal. These are a bunch of real weirdos here." Pete pointed at us as if we were an exhibit of what it meant to be inhuman.

So why do we deserve your attention if we're so weird?" Charlotte Ann asked.

"Hey, Pete. Y'all gonna get the creepin' crud standin' so close to us," Bobby Jo intoned. That broke me up and I started to giggle. Then Charlotte Ann started to laugh. In the middle of our laughing, Pete left, Scotty pushing him away from us.

"Thanks, Scotty," I said when I found him by his locker at the end of the day. "Thanks for taking care of Pete. And thanks for helping me get people for our club last week."

"Sure, Meredith. Pete can get pretty obnoxious." We started to walk out together toward the parking lot. The sky was somber and a moist chill shivered my neck. I wasn't sure whether to keep pace with Scotty, but I did, every silent second making me feel he had not meant to walk side by side with me. I had almost convinced myself to fall back, or find some excuse to leave his company when he spoke. "Would you like to see a gymkhana?"

It took a second to understand Scotty was talking to me and that he was speaking English. "A what?"

"A gymkhana. It's games and contests on horseback. You compete in races. They're a lot of fun."

"But I can hardly stay on a horse," I said. "I hated the riding lessons. I got worse instead of better." I didn't like admitting this to Scotty, but I didn't tell him that I loved playing tennis as much as I disliked horseback riding just to get credit for being okay at something. After the hard time he'd had trying to teach me how to hold a racket, I wasn't about to make myself out as a skilled tennis player. I wanted to surprise him someday.

"You don't have to ride, Meredith. You'd watch me and other girls and guys our age compete. It's February sixteenth. There's a dance after, with a country and western band. We're a club too."

I smiled. "More organized than ours?"

"I guess." He laughed.

My knees felt weak. "Sure. It sounds exciting."

"Ask your mom and let me know. Gotta go." He ran toward his brother's shiny red truck.

"Scotty," I shouted. He stopped. "I'm sorry I was such an ass when you tried to teach me tennis."

"No problem."

The whole parking lot heard me call myself an ass. Weirdo. Ass. I didn't care. I almost threw my books high into the air and shouted, "He likes me!"

Chapter • 11 •

"Hi, Mr. McGee. I'm Scott Dumont." Scotty reached out his hand. "And Mrs. McGee. It's nice to meet you." Would I have such poise in another year? I wondered. Probably not. "This is my brother, Buff."

We were all standing around the living room, me, my mom and dad, Scotty and Buff. I wished Grandma were there, and I smiled to myself, because I had this funny thought that she'd absolutely die at the sight of Scotty and his brother, each in a plaid shirt, jeans and boots, with cowboy hat in hand, waiting to whisk me away. "Where's your mom and dad?" I asked. I had expected that Scotty's parents would be picking me up.

"Dad's getting the riding ring ready, and Mom's helping set up the food for the party afterward. They'll bring you back. Would midnight be too late?" He looked at my parents. "My folks will have to stay and help clean up."

"That seems awfully late." It was the first time I'd seen my father so uncertain.

"Midnight's fine this once," Mom said. "Have fun." I squeezed her hand tight.

Dad kissed me on the cheek. "You look great."

92

"Thanks, Daddy." I was wearing boots, a pale pink and baby-blue plaid cowboy shirt, a navy blue down vest, and some great new blue jeans.

"Don't get on any wild horses though. Your pants will rip."

"Daddy, ssh." I quickly moved out the doorway and across the yard to the truck. Buff already had the engine running and Scotty was holding the door. I was trembling all over. It was my first real dance. Scotty would have to take my hand just like Jeannie used to when we practiced in Chicago. I wondered how I'd feel then.

I climbed into the truck and found plenty of space in the middle. "This is my first time in a truck," I said before I could stop myself. Was I really going to say things that weird all night?

"Do you like it?" Scotty asked.

"Sure."

"Buff's worked real hard to get it. It's his pride and joy. After Linda Beth."

"You own her too?" I asked.

They both laughed. "No," Buff said. "She's my girlfriend. She's got my promise ring though."

"You know already you're going to get married?" I asked, still thinking that he talked about the truck and Linda Beth as though they weren't really that different.

"Pretty much. But not till after college."

When we picked up Linda Beth I could see one reason why Buff had given her a promise ring. She was absolutely luscious, with long jet black hair, long fingernails like Tina's and snow white skin. I knew five years of aging and curving would never be that kind to me.

Pressed between Linda Beth and Scotty, I was silent for most of the fifteen-minute drive to the stables and riding ring, listening and laughing while the other three talked. I was curious about

Linda Beth and Buff, though, so I asked, "How long have you two known each other?"

Linda Beth turned her big brown eyes to Buff and then back to me. "I guess since we were twelve. We've been going to these gymkhanas since then, right?"

"Right," Buff said.

I found all this very interesting. Buff and Linda Beth had been going to gymkhanas together since they were twelve. Now at seventeen Linda Beth had a promise ring. I thought about Tina in love at fifteen. Such things would never happen to me. I figured I wouldn't date until I was twenty-five. Or eighty-five. That was a joke I made when Jeannie asked me when I thought I'd go on my first date. Charlotte Ann and I hadn't talked too much about that kind of thing. Was this a date? Could I call this my first date? Nope. I wouldn't.

The stables were cool, and I was glad I was wearing my down vest. Mr. Dumont was still raking out the ring. "I'm glad to meet you, Meredith." He gave me a strong, sinewy hand. He looked a lot like Scotty, only his brown curly hair had no red in it, and he was taller, more weathered. "Is this your first gymkhana?"

"Yes, sir."

"They're real exciting. They can be dangerous, but we supervise things pretty closely. We don't want Scotty getting hurt, do we?"

"Oh, no." What else could I say? I liked Scotty. I liked him a lot.

"Come meet Lucifer." Scotty moved away, reaching out his hand toward me. Instinctively I took it. I had never taken a boy's hand before except in a square-dancing class in Chicago. That was a pretty humiliating experience, because I had gotten my finger smashed in a car door and the nail decided to fall off right in the middle of the class, right into Charlie Ferguson's hand.

But this was different. Once I had taken Scotty's hand I wondered if I should let go and when I was supposed to let go. I had never had so many uninvited questions race through my head.

When we got to Lucifer's stall, Scotty let go of my hand just as naturally as he had taken it. "This is Lucifer. Lucifer, meet Meredith."

"Hi, Lucifer." Lucifer was pitch black with a white, starlike mark on his forehead. I petted his face and combed his forelock with my fingers. "Is he all yours?"

"Yeah. Dad got him for me last year."

Then I watched while Scotty saddled Lucifer. The stables began to fill with people and horses and anticipation.

"Here. You might need this, since you'll be sitting still. I'm already starting to sweat." Scotty handed me his denim jacket. "You better get a seat."

I took a seat midway up the bleachers, and Linda Beth soon joined me.

"Aren't you riding?" I asked.

"Not anymore. I think it's all too dangerous."

I started to bite my fingernails, but with Linda Beth sitting next to me, I changed to wringing Scotty's jacket. There was a keyhole race, a figure-eight stake race, and then came the barrel race.

"Scotty's great at this. Let's go down front."

I followed Linda Beth. So far I had seen Scotty compete twice, and I was glad to get a closer look. The place was wild with excitement and tension, and about half the spectators had already left the bleachers for the railing.

Apparently everyone knew Scotty's reputation, because the crowd grew quiet when it was his turn. The gun suddenly exploded the crowd's dramatic hush. I shivered. The crowd inched forward, tight against the rough-hewn fence. My hands gripped the railing and held fast as dust spiraled into the air above the arena. Lucifer's tail and forelock flew, red glints magically appearing in his shiny, jet coat, Scotty's hair afire in the glaring arena light. Scotty and Lucifer sped forward like a bullet. The course seemed very complex to me. How could he remember it?

Without looking right or left, Lucifer charged straightaway between two enormous, padded barrels. At the last minute, with invisible guidance, he headed west and, like a fast-spinning cyclone, circled counterclockwise, catching himself then to fly dead away east, there making a clockwise pirouette, dust smoldering in all directions, before he charged dead-center up the arena. There was another clockwise circle so tight I was sure Scotty would lose a leg. He wasn't even grazed. They took the final straightaway at breakneck speed. The cloverleaf was engraved in a shower of dust, amid a storm of cheers.

Had Scotty won the barrel race? I didn't know. My heart and body fluttered with excitement. Maybe this was what Mom felt when men reminded her of Rhett Butler. I clung to the rail, stunned, and a few minutes later went to find Scotty to tell him congratulations.

When I finally found him, he was surrounded by a bunch of guys all slapping him on the back, nudging him, rubbing Lucifer's neck. I figured this was how they behaved in the locker room in the gym. Sometimes you could hear them through the door. I pretended not to be interested, but I was inwardly very attentive.

"Grub's on," someone shouted. Slowly the group dwindled.

"You can go with them if you want, Meredith. I think there's chili and jalapeño cornbread."

"I'll wait for you. Can I help?"

"Sure. You can help rub down Lucifer." He gave me a cloth. "Hope you don't mind getting a little stinky?"

"Who me?" Smells like Lucifer's had been known to make me choke. Rubbing him down seemed a lot like shining black shoes, except there was sweat. I had become quite used to sweat, though, since we moved south. My sweat that is. Mom had finally bought me some deodorant that plugged up my armpits. I stopped rubbing Lucifer for a second, resting my arms. It was hard work. I watched Scotty carefully brush a liquid on Lucifer's hooves, making them shiny. "Are you painting his toenails?"

"Sort of. This stuff protects his hooves. Like hand lotion, I guess. Or polish."

"I think purple's Lucifer's shade. Huh, Lucifer? Black and purple."

"With glitter on the top?"

"Yeah," I said. "Can you imagine that?"

"Sure can. But we won't do it to you, Lucifer. We'll let Meredith get Lucinda and *she* can get all decked out like that."

Scotty led Lucifer back into his stall. "Now don't kick any wood chips and manure at Meredith. She's had her fill." I pushed Scotty and he laughed. "You'll never live it down, Meredith. At least not with me."

"You were really great tonight, Scotty."

"Thanks."

I was relaxed and happy. I met his mom and found out where Scotty gets the red in his hair. She was soft and pale, and a little chubby. I liked her right away, the way I do some people.

The music was loud. We took a seat by the fireplace to eat. The few pieces of furniture in the lodge had been moved back and wide oak planks were vibrating to the music and to the stamping and tapping of feet. The chili was spicy, and I figured I was going to smell like a ranch hand by the end of the evening. Then Scotty asked me to dance.

"I can't dance what everyone's dancing."

"Come on, Meredith." He stretched out his hand farther. "You can dance. You can dance the Cotton-Eyed Joe." He pulled me onto the floor.

At first I had a hard time. But when I stopped expecting something and started paying attention to his way, I suddenly caught on. Soon I was laughing, even at my mistakes. And by the end of the evening I had learned the Cotton-Eyed Joe.

Mr. and Mrs. Dumont took me home at about eleven-thirty. Scotty walked me to the front door. I didn't think I was going to get a good-night kiss, and I was right. We shook hands.

When he was halfway down the sidewalk, Scotty turned and called to me, watching him from the doorway. "I almost forgot. Happy Valentine's Day."

"Thanks." I waved. "Same to you. See you Monday."

February 16

Dear Grandma,

I just realized I haven't written in two weeks. Sorry.

Can you believe it? I just got back from my first date. Well, not really. But close. I had a lot of fun. But you know what? I'm embarrassed to see Scotty at school on Monday. A little afraid too. What if he doesn't pay any attention to me, as if this never happened?

I'm so excited I don't think I'll be able to sleep.

Love,
Meredith

Lots of times when I close my eyes to sleep I see Grandma's face. But that night I saw Scotty and Lucifer.

Chapter · 12 ·

Scotty didn't pay me any special attention that next Monday. Or any other day, for that matter. We were friendly, but nothing special. Maybe I was expecting things to be too much like the movies. Maybe I was being extra-sensitive as he'd said on the tennis court that Sunday. But his lack of attention confused me and hurt too. I decided, then and there, that I would not make the tennis team for him (because he'd never notice anyway), but for myself. Doing something just for me didn't decrease my drive, though. It increased it, like a charge of dynamite or one of my fireballs.

One Saturday that spring, just when the bluebonnets were turning the fields along the highway into seas of blue, richer and deeper than the sky, Dad and I set out for the tennis courts. It was eight in the morning, and I wanted to practice my serve for hours on end—or for as long as my father was willing to return balls. Then I was going to relax and write Grandma to explain how busy I'd been and fill her in on all the details she'd missed, especially what Charlotte Ann had to say about me and Scotty.

We'd gone to see a movie at the mall that Friday night, and waiting for the movie to start I'd asked her a silly question.

"Charlotte Ann?"

"Yup."

"You know that time two months ago when I went to the gymkhana with Scotty?"

"Yeah."

"Do you think that was a date?"

"Why do you care whether it was a date or not?" she had asked.

Charlotte Ann was like that, able to poke questions right where they hurt. Some part of her toughness had softened, but not that part of her. I didn't feel she meant to hurt me though. "I don't know. I guess because he hasn't paid any attention to me at all since then."

"It's basketball season."

"Yeah, but when I'm at a game or watch a practice, he hardly says more than hello."

"Are you going to 'yeah but' everything I say?"

I wanted to tell her "Yes," but I had just smiled and shrugged.

"He's only thirteen, Meredith. Maybe fourteen. You're only twelve."

"What about Romeo and Juliet?"

"Even they were probably older."

"Yeah, but what do you think?"

"It wasn't a date. He probably likes you but it wasn't a date." Her conclusion had made me feel good. "I'm glad."

"That he likes you?"

"No. That it wasn't a date. I didn't want it to be a date."

"Why?"

"I don't want to date till I'm sixteen."

"That's a long way away."

"I know it's a long way away. I want boys to like me in between now and then. I just don't want to date. Besides, if that was a date and this is how a boy acts afterward, I don't think I ever want to date."

"I don't think you have to worry much about going out before you're sixteen."

For that comment I had given her a punch. Luckily we didn't spill any of our popcorn.

"Meredith! Come on now, concentrate!" My father's loud encouragement stopped my daydream. "That's more like it," he shouted as I gave him my best serve ever. And I kept up the good work for nearly forty-five minutes.

That's when my mother came to the park. She sat down on the closest bench. I figured she'd brought us a snack. Then I saw that what she held in her lap wasn't food. It was my notebook, the notebook that held all my letters to Grandma. Part of me was surprised, but part wasn't at all. It seemed all these months I'd sort of been waiting for, and dreading, the discovery.

"A good time for a break," my dad said. He took the towel we had draped over the net and wiped the sweat from the back of his neck and the bridge of his nose where his sunglasses sat. He took a swig of water from our thermos and headed toward my mother. "Where's Adam?" He put his sunglasses back on and looked around.

I didn't move. I stood behind the service line, waiting to see what was going to happen next. I felt nervous, almost sick, that kind of sick I get when I'm feeling guilty but don't quite understand what I've done that's so wrong. And I felt a little too angry at my mother to move closer to her. The letters were mine, they were my secret, and she had invaded my privacy.

"He's watching cartoons and Sarah's watching him," my mother explained. Sarah's an older woman in our neighborhood who does babysitting. "I thought it might be a good change for just the three of us to talk without all of Adam's whooping and hollering." She looked over at me. I hadn't budged an inch and I still felt sick. "They're beautiful letters, Meredith."

"They're private," I said.

"What are you two talking about?" My dad looked from Mom to me. I shook my head no, to say I didn't want to talk about anything now, especially my letters.

"While I was cleaning I found the letters Meredith has been writing to Grandma."

"To my mother?" my dad said. I could tell he was confused. And that he'd never understand. Neither of them would ever understand. I turned and started to run from them.

"Meredith, wait!" my mother shouted. "We need to talk."

I stopped and faced her. She was standing, ready to run after me, her cheeks red. "They're beautiful, honey, like poetry really."

"But that's *my* room and *my* drawer! I didn't give you permission to go through my things. Nothing needed cleaning in my bottom drawer."

"I know, Meredith."

"Then why did you snoop?" I could feel my voice rise in protest and my shoulders tighten, but part of me didn't feel angry. Most of me felt sad and relieved, as if I wanted to burst into tears and have my mother comfort me. At least she saw my letters as beautiful.

"I wasn't snooping, Meredith. Really I wasn't. It was an accident. I was sorting spring clothes to send to Tina. I found some of your pajamas mixed up with her things and was just putting them back where they belong."

"Oh." Some of the wind was taken out of me, and now I didn't know what to do.

"Why don't you come over here, Meredith?" my dad suggested, "and explain to me what's going on. Grandma's been dead nearly ten months."

"Well, I know that," I said. I went and stood nearer my folks, but not too close.

My father reached for my notebook.

"Don't," I said.

"Let me see what Mom's talking about." He opened to the first page. I watched him smile. He turned a page and kept reading. Then he tilted his head in a funny way, flipped through all the pages to see how much lay ahead of him, and sat down on the bench next to Mom. I got that same sick feeling in my stomach I get when a teacher starts to hand out test papers and does it very slowly.

I couldn't imagine my parents would give me approval for the letters, like with a good grade. But I'd die if they did the complete opposite.

"I loved writing the letters," I said. "Is there something wrong with that?"

"You must have thought there was something wrong," Dad said, "or you wouldn't have hid them."

They were going to spoil everything. "They're private. That's all. Like a diary," I said. "But I guess I did feel there was something wrong with me that I couldn't stop writing." I felt helpless and wanted to run like when I'd heard about Tina going away to school. I hated feeling this helpless. I wished one of them would come and hug me and say everything was going to be okay.

And then I saw it. A tear running down my father's cheek. "You loved her as much as I did," he said. "Maybe more. There's nothing wrong with that, Meredith." He smiled. His face couldn't decide whether to laugh or cry.

"I never saw you cry when Grandma died," I said as I came closer. His not crying had made me think that there was something wrong with how sad I felt.

"I didn't want to scare you," he said, "so when I did cry I hid it." He paused. "Am I scaring you now?"

"Yeah," I said. "But not because you're crying. I'm afraid 'cause of them." I nodded at my notebook.

Everything was quiet then. My father kept turning pages, my mother looking over his shoulder. I hit a few serves and tried a volley against the backboard, but I couldn't concentrate. When I looked at them again, Mom had both her arms linked through Dad's left arm. They looked sort of cozy.

My father closed the notebook, set it on the bench next to him, and took a deep breath. Then he blew his nose. "What do we do?" He looked at my mother.

"I don't know," my mother said. "I think *we* should be punished."

"Why?" This wasn't a totally new idea to me, but I'd sure never heard *them* say anything like it.

"We let you down," she said. "We could have talked more about Grandma's dying, what death means. We should have helped with your questions, and your hurt. Or at least tried. We could have listened. We should have listened."

"I didn't give you much of a chance," I said. "I kind of figured I shouldn't hurt so much."

"But she was your grandmother," Mom said. "No wonder your feelings are so strong. You're sad because you loved her so much and now she's gone forever."

I shrugged, trying to shrug off what she'd said, but I couldn't and I started to cry.

"But she's not gone," I said. "I think I'll feel her always, like she was here."

My mother's eyes filled with tears too. She reached out her free arm and pulled me close. "I know what you mean," she said. "I love you like that." How much I needed to hear that!

I saw another tear creep down from under my father's sun-glasses. So there we sat, all in a line, cuddled together and crying. I was glad Adam wasn't around. I wouldn't want to scare him with just how weird all the older people in his family were.

Suddenly I realized I wasn't all that different from my father. I was scared of letting others see how I really felt. Everyone, that is, except Grandma.

"I don't completely understand all this," my father finally said. "I think we've got a lot to talk about and work out. Maybe your mother's right. I know I'm sorry I didn't communicate, Meredith. I guess I thought if I showed you what I felt I'd be showing you a weak man for a father. I wanted to protect you. And it was tough to talk about death."

We sat for a long time, until all our tears had dried and we were ready to go home. But no one had come to any conclusion about my letters, least of all me.

The fried chicken we had that night was the best food I'd ever eaten. Even though the air was chilly, I went out on the patio with Mom to watch the stars while she drank her coffee. Dad came out and held Adam.

"Can I still write my letters?" I asked. "You won't make me stop, will you?"

"Until you've said everything you want to say, I don't suppose there's really much we can do," Mom said.

"But we are concerned," my dad said, "about your using this way of communicating, and eventually closing yourself off from us and others. And I wonder, too, whether the letters aren't a hand-icap."

"A handicap?" I was puzzled.

He nodded. "Maybe they're keeping you from finally accept-ing Grandma's death."

"I guess they sort of let me pretend she's still around."

He nodded. "In a way they're a screen you use that doesn't let you face the facts. But sometimes I feel her near, too, honey. Like the way she loved the Chicago Cubs. All last summer I used to go to the phone to call her about their latest performance. Then I'd have to stop and think that she was gone for good and would never share another good baseball story."

"Let's take some more time to think about all this," my mother said. "Maybe we can talk in the morning."

I felt quiet and thoughtful, anyway, not wanting to talk anymore. I lay back and watched the stars come softly, brilliantly alive within the immense blackness. I wondered if they each felt lonely in all that dark space. For some reason, maybe the beauty and the peace of it all, I imagined that they didn't. And maybe, when you truly live like a starry sparkle, the way Grandma did, you're not lonely or bothered by being alone. Or maybe you're not even afraid to die.

My eyelids grew heavy. It was like a fountain of relief to have the letters out in the open and to be finally able to talk about it all.

Chapter · 13 ·

I woke with a start from a dream that my letters to Grandma were being burned in an enormous bonfire. I threw my underwear from its drawer and found the butterfly notebook, nearly full now, undisturbed.

April 19

Dear Grandma,

Mom found the letters yesterday. I was hoping they'd always be secret, but I guess I figured something like this would have to happen. I mean, I like writing and all, staying in touch. But can you imagine me having to explain this to my husband? "Are you ready to go out to eat? Not yet dear. I'm writing a letter. 'Oh, to whom?' To my grandmother. 'Oh, when can I meet her?' "

So, I figured I'd stop sometime. I even hope I do. But I don't feel like stopping right now. I don't know why. I'm just not ready, any more ready than Adam is to give up Baby Cat.

Love,
Mama Cat

I didn't quite understand what I had written. Was I thinking about saying goodbye? Goodbye for good? What did that mean anyway? I lay back in bed till I heard breakfast noises.

I found Mom in the kitchen. "Hey, Mom," I whispered. "What did you decide?" I was anxious to know. I felt I certainly still needed to write letters to Grandma.

"We'll talk about it over breakfast. How about pancakes?"

"Sure." Actually, nothing sounded good with this discussion up in the air.

"We're thinking," Mom began, once she'd finished eating and was slowly sipping coffee, "that maybe you'd like to talk to someone about the letters and why you need to write them. And about Grandma dying. Someone other than us."

"Like whom?" I asked.

"A counselor," Dad said.

"A what?"

"A counselor," Adam repeated.

"Thanks." I stared at him and he giggled.

"You're welcome."

"I'm not that weird. Can't we try something else? Maybe if I just talk to you guys." All I could think of was Mr. Howard at school. If the counselor Mom was talking about was anything like Mr. Howard, I was doomed.

"I don't think you're weird," Dad said. "I just don't think we can take this lightly. It's serious, for you and for us."

"I won't give up my letter-writing for anybody," I said. I was feeling nervous again. If I gave up writing the letters, I wanted to do it for myself and no one else.

"We're not asking you to," Dad said. "But maybe someone else can help better than us."

"I don't think so," I said. "And I won't have any practice time if I'm seeing some old counselor. Tennis is more important to me than anything."

"I think this is more important," Mom said. "We have to keep the lines of communication open."

"You just said *we* have to talk. Why get a counselor involved?" I asked.

"Well, maybe you're right, Meredith," Mom said slowly and thoughtfully. "It is our problem. We're the ones who need to talk. Maybe because Tina's deaf, we haven't talked enough, somehow. We'll try it your way, and we'll keep it in the family. But we expect you to talk with us about what's on your mind. We can't listen unless you talk."

"And I want to hear your ideas," I said. Then I thought of something. "You won't snoop, will you?" I asked.

Mom shook her head no, but Dad said, "We'll have to take it one step at a time and do whatever's best."

"Maybe I don't like what's best," I said.

"Maybe sometimes I don't either," he said, very matter-of-factly. There was in that moment some truth between my father and me that made me feel I would become an adult someday. It was a kind of certainty.

What happened then was more fun than I expected. From that day on, Mom, Dad, and I, even Adam, chatted away about Grandma. We talked about our favorite times with her. I taught Dad the stories she used to tell, and he started a storytime with Adam right before bed. He even began making up his own stories, too. I got to listen if my homework was done, and I learned my dad had some of the same storytelling talent as Grandma. That made sense to me. After all, she was his mother.

When I was alone with them, my folks talked about death and dying. I think my mom even did some research, because she sud-

denly had a stack of books from the library by her side of the bed.
Most were about different religions. There were a few about death
itself, and two by women who said they talked with God. But I
was much more interested in what conclusions they'd come to on
their own, not the things they'd learned from others.

"I don't think people die completely," I said as we talked over
dessert. Adam was already in the yard, playing with our cat.

"Oh," my father said as he took his last bite of pecan pie, "and
what is it exactly that they do?" He was sort of teasing me, and
sort of serious.

"Well . . ." I looked at my mother.

"Go ahead, honey. You've thought about this a lot more than
me and I'm three times your age." Dad looked at her and she
smiled. "*Easily* three times your age."

"Well," I began, "their love and good works stay behind. It's
why I disagree with that part from the Bible about not building
up your treasure on earth. It depends on what you mean by
treasure."

"I think I understand," my mother said. "In a way, you were
your Grandma's treasure."

"I didn't mean it like that," I said. But I realized my mother
did understand, and in her own way, not in a way she'd read in
books.

"And that's why you feel Grandma's still here," she added.
"Because she loved you a lot. You were her heart's treasure.
You'll always be that, whether or not you write the letters."

I nodded again, but this time a lump in my throat got in the
way. I couldn't talk. Remembering what my grandmother meant
to me, and me to her, only made me sad. I'd lost a lot when
Grandma died.

And then something suddenly dawned on me, without anybody saying anything more. I felt a quiet voice way down deep

inside. I could look at it all differently. I could look at all I'd gained from Grandma. I could look at how she put riches in my life just by being good company and by loving me. She'd colored my life more than any rainbow ever colored the sky.

"But people do die, Meredith," my father said. "There's a finality . . ."

"She talks to me," I said before I knew what I meant.

"She talks to you?" my father said.

"In a way," I said. "Maybe it's my imagination. But she talks to me here," I pointed to my heart, "and in everything I like to do, and how I do it. So do you." I looked at my parents. "Love stays. It never dies, Daddy." I felt about to burst inside. I wanted to dance, to sing, to hug.

"Okay. So you're telling me Grandma did die," my father said, "but her love didn't?"

I smiled. Parents! He could put it that way if he wanted, but I wouldn't. "You could say that." But me? I couldn't separate my grandmother from her love.

"But do you need the letters then?" my mother asked. "If Grandma's love does stay, then why do you need something physical like the letters? Isn't love enough?"

"That's a good question, Mom." I didn't know the answer, but I felt I was getting closer.

"You know, Meredith," she said. "Mac and I love you very much."

I smiled. "I know." But hearing her say that felt like the sun coming through after the storm.

I got some more help at school when Ms. Bryant decided our English class needed some practice in public speaking.

"I figure it'll take a week to go around the room," she announced one Friday afternoon, "but I want everyone prepared on Monday to talk about the most important person in their life. The topic's really simple, and I really don't want you to spend a lot of time preparing. I want you to concentrate on the speaking techniques we've discussed and not so much on content."

I knew my most important person was Grandma, but I wasn't at all sure I could talk about her in front of my class. I might cry. I sat in my desk until all the other kids had left, telling Charlotte Ann I had a question for Ms. Bryant and not to wait.

"I don't think I can do this, Ms. Bryant," I said, trying to get her attention as she erased the blackboard. Luckily she didn't have a class that next period.

"You'll do fine, Meredith," she said. "You participate in class as much as anyone."

"It's not the speaking. It's the topic."

"Surely there's somebody . . ."

"My grandmother was the most important person, and she's dead."

"That's okay. The person doesn't have to be living."

I shook my head. "No, no it isn't."

She turned and looked at me. "I'm sorry I said that," she said. "Of course it isn't okay. It's hard when someone you love dies."

I nodded. "I'm afraid I might cry. Crying isn't part of public speaking."

"Hmmm," she said. "I think it is."

"What?"

"Well, public speaking happens lots of different ways. And sometimes speakers are moved to tears for lots of different reasons."

"Maybe I should just talk about someone else."

"I'd tell the truth, Meredith, if I were you, and see what happens," she said. "What's the worst that can happen?"

"I'd cry and they'd laugh." I looked back at the empty class-room, imagining my classmates.

"I don't think you give them enough credit. I think they'd un-derstand that you loved your grandmother very much."

"I did," I said. "I write her letters even now. That's how much I miss her." I explained to her about my notebook and she didn't bat an eye.

"Maybe you're meant to be a writer," she said. "Writing let-ters is an art, just like good public speaking. Why don't you try, Meredith?"

I sighed. She was just like all my teachers. "I guess."

She looked at me closely. "I've never done this before." She paused.

"Done what, Ms. Bryant?"

She took a slip of paper from her top desk drawer. "Here's my home phone number if you need encouragement over the week-end."

I folded it inside my English book. "Thanks." I started to leave.

"When did your grandmother die?" she asked.

"Back in June. June second."

"It takes time to grieve and say goodbye, Meredith. Longer than most people think. Were you with her when she died?"

"No, not in person. The last few days I couldn't go to the hospital. I guess that's because of how she looked or something. I really don't know. But I wasn't allowed to go then."

"Why, you never got a chance to say a final goodbye. No wonder you write the letters."

I smiled. "Yeah, but I've got to stop sometime."

"I sometimes think acceptance is the hardest thing asked of us as human beings, especially when someone we love is gone for good. When you can accept her leaving, then I don't think you'll need the letters."

I never needed to call Ms. Bryant that weekend. I felt she understood me, and somehow that was enough.

Ms. Bryant drew our names out of a cigar box rather than have us go in alphabetical order. As luck would have it, I had my turn that Monday.

I did cry, just a little, but then Jason Wakefield fainted and Bonnie Sylvester looked as if she was either going to cry from fear or vomit so there wasn't any reason to feel bad. I wasn't sorry at all for my performance, except that at the end, when everybody clapped, I was the only one who took a bow. Then they all laughed. It was the ham in me, I guess, but it was hard not to hear the applause and take credit.

As I was leaving class Ms. Bryant called me over to her desk. "You were quite an inspiration today."

I smiled. "It was fun. And it kept my mind off what's going to happen Friday."

"What's that?"

"Tennis team tryouts."

"Oh," she said. "Well, good luck."

"Thanks." I turned to leave.

"Just remember, Meredith. Life flows, full of changes, like a big, wide river with lots of bends. It's hard to see that when you're young."

"And I'm just floating along like baby Moses?"

She smiled. "That's how it is. Sometimes all you can do is trust."

"Have you ever heard of a person having a fountain inside?" I asked. I figured Ms. Bryant had probably read more than anyone I knew.

"Why, everything about you is a fountain," she said. "If you really let it flow, you're a never-ending fountain of all you're meant to be."

I liked the idea of the fountain being never ending. I was pretty sure I would feel my own grandmother with me whether or not I wrote letters to her, just as Mom had said. "You know, I'm still writing the letters to my grandmother."

"When the time is right, you'll give them up. Good luck on Friday."

"I'm as ready as I can be."

Chapter • 14 •

I could hardly sleep the Thursday night before tennis team tryouts. I tossed and turned. And then something woke me early. I wasn't sure what. All I could feel was a cool breeze, like the cool breezes that bring change.

"When do you try out, honey?" Dad kissed me on the forehead and took a quick gulp of coffee. I was trying to eat a bowl of cereal without much success. I felt too nervous to swallow.

"During gym. We'll go into lunch period if we need extra time."

"When's that?"

"Ten-thirty to twelve-thirty."

"I have a conference with a Canadian oil company then. But I'll be thinking of you. Have you got your visor?"

"Yup. And Mom's lucky flannel shirt."

"Well, good luck." He gave me another kiss, what he called a good-luck kiss, flung on his suit jacket, and was out the door. I knew that as busy as he was going to be, he'd keep his eye on the clock and think of me at just the right time.

"You'll do real well, Meredith." At the other end of the table Mom put down the newspaper. Since all the talk about Grandma, my parents treated me more like a person, like an adult. Anyway, they took more notice of me and I felt more like my own person, not just someone stuck in the middle between Tina and Adam.

"Thanks, Mom."

When I was ready to go out the door Adam came running. He gave me a frosted flakes kiss and said, "Good luck, Mama Cat."

"How do you feel?" Charlotte Ann grabbed my elbow as I made my way from the bus to my locker. "Geez, you feel like ice."

"I'm a little nervous."

"Well, I know something that won't help. Pete says he's going to put you right on your rear."

"What?"

"You know how he talks."

"Does that mean *he's* playing me?"

"I guess."

I felt dejected.

"Don't worry," Charlotte Ann said. "It's how you play, not whether you win. You'll get on the team. Maybe I'm wrong about his playing you. And maybe you'll beat him."

Maybe, I thought, but probably not. She had probably not misunderstood him. And I probably wouldn't win. I had the jitters all through homeroom, English, and Texas History, and went to the bathroom every time I passed one in the hall.

When we got to the gym I felt so cold and shaky I could hardly dress.

"Here, let me straighten that." Charlotte Ann had brought a yellow headband from her grandmother for good luck. "You look cute," she said stepping away from me and taking a good look.

"You don't win with cute."

"Maybe it'll help. Maybe old Petie will see you and just melt."

"Maybe." I thought for a moment. "How'd you two get to be so different?"

"We just are. You know what, Meredith?"

"What? He's adopted?"

"No." Charlotte Ann laughed. "Grandma wants to go up to the state school to visit Joanna and maybe bring her home for the summer. Mom said she'd love that. Pete had a fit. Do you want to come with us and meet her?"

"Sure. If it's okay."

"I wouldn't ask if it wasn't okay. Anyway, you know more about this kind of stuff than we do. You'd be a big help."

"Sure," I said flipping my tennis racket up in the air. "I just go with the flow."

Charlotte Ann squeezed my hand for good luck. I felt an easiness then, a sense of everything being all right with the world, no matter what happened. Until I saw Pete. And Scotty.

"Hi," I said to Scotty.

"Hi, Meredith. How are you doing?"

"I'm pretty nervous."

"Well, good luck."

"Thanks. Are you watching?"

"Yeah. I'm next year's captain."

"Congratulations."

"Yup. He's taking over my place," Pete said as he walked up and stood, one foot resting on the bench beside us. He looked crisp and confident. "Ready, Meredith?"

"Sure. Do I play you?"

"You bet."

Pete won the first serve and I thought he sneered, but I could have been mistaken. He seemed to be the kind of person who took pleasure in other people's failure.

We took our places across the net, Pete swaggering more than stepping. Wham! The serve came over, straight as a missile targeted for my throat. I thought of every nasty thing he had ever said and done to Charlotte Ann and me. Whoosh, I sent the ball back, just inches over the net. Off-guard, he stumbled back. My point. Pete's eyes narrowed. Up went the toss, all his motion deceptively relaxed. Because around came his racket at top speed and then slam. I had the ball again. Muscles in my upper arm reacted.

Pete's backhand caught the deep corner ball and he hammered one at me. Up I lobbed the yellow bullet. It sailed high, its color exploding in the midday sun. He stepped back, shaded his eyes, and let it fly right at me. I hit it back, weakly, just over the net again, too wobbly and small a return for Pete to keep the ball in play. My point.

My left eyebrow guided a drop of sweat away from my eye and down my temple to my cheek. I couldn't afford that kind of ticklish distraction. I felt like a tiger licking its chops while watching its prey as I stretched my tongue for the salty bead. I had never felt so determined, or so strong.

I won the first two games and Pete won the third.

"Okay," Scotty yelled. "That's enough. You're on the team, Meredith."

I heard a cheer and turned. Charlotte Ann was there after all, behind the fence. She clapped and blew me a kiss. "See you at lunch."

I waved. "Thanks," I mouthed. "Save me a seat." She hurried off as the bell rang.

"We've got to do a set," Pete yelled.

"We never do a set," Scotty protested. "There isn't time."

"There's time," Pete said.

I lost the next three games. At the end I walked up and shook Pete's hand. "Good luck in high school," I said. "Did you make the team there?"

"Yup. Thanks, Meredith. You played a good game."

"Thanks."

I didn't much mind losing. I would have minded missing lunch, but thankfully I had half an hour left. Our club was still meeting at the same table and I couldn't wait to tell everyone I'd made the team. I started to jog back to the locker room.

"Meredith," Scotty called out.

I stopped. "Yeah?"

"Congratulations." He walked toward me.

"Thanks."

"You'll be great to have on the team. We practice all summer."

"I know."

"Do you want to play some tomorrow?"

"Sure."

"I'll call you."

"Okay." I started to walk away, though I felt like staying with him for a long time.

"And my brother's having a party," he quickly added. "Do you remember Buff?"

"Sure. From the gymkhana." I could have told him I remembered all that like it happened yesterday.

He smiled and nodded. "Right. Well, he's graduating from high school a week from tomorrow."

"That's great. Linda Beth too?"

"Yeah. My folks are having a big party that Saturday night. Do you want to come?"

"Sure."

"Great. Is it a date then?"

"I'll have to check with my mom first. I'll let you know tomorrow."

"Okay. I'll call."

He had already said he would call, but I really didn't mind hearing it a second time.

Everyone at the lunch table was thrilled to hear my news about making the tennis team. I didn't tell anyone about Buff's party and Scotty inviting me.

By the time I got off the bus after school I could hardly wait to tell Mom and Dad about the tennis team. And to tell Charlotte Ann and Tina about Scotty asking me to Buff's party and wanting to practice tennis with me, too. I thought about all the people in my life now for a minute, without all the noise of school. Just that cool breeze of change around me. Spring. Summer.

And then, on the walk from the bus stop to the house, I talked to Grandma. I told her I could sense her, like a never-ending, flowing presence all around. I told her that I loved her, that I always had and always would. She was the most important person in my life so far and I could never say goodbye to all she meant to me. I didn't need to write her. Her love and joy would be with me always.

The spring breeze sighed, gentle, cool and soothing. I broke into a run. The wind met my tears and carried them away. Suddenly the day was misty gold. A quiet joy bubbled from a fountain that knew no beginning, no end.

"Hey, Mom!" I shouted. "I'm home."